THE
RANKIN FILES

Dan Malone

Set up and cover design by:

www.gondorwriterscentre.com

THE
RANKIN FILES

ISBN: 978-0-9876353-1-0

www.gondorwriterscentre.com

CHAPTER 1

TABLELANDS MURDERS

Rankin jogged up the stairs of the State Police Headquarters in Brisbane, glancing to his right at the sandstone building that housed the police academy. He had graduated as a constable there eighteen years ago. It had been a hard grind through the ranks where seniority had then outranked ability. Fast tracked through the upper ranks to Homicide Chief Inspector, the pressure was now on him to get results quickly to keep his promotion. The new Commissioner would be watching closely.

He was now Chief Inspector of the elite State Homicide Squad. He answered only to the recently appointed Police Commissioner, Jason Wirth. Rankin's old boss in the arson squad, Larson, was now Deputy Commissioner. Brady, the CIB Chief had retired. William Turner was now CIB chief. It was a new era for the police.

It was a step up for Rankin, previously a team member. Now he had to find the self-confidence to motivate and manage the elite State Homicide Squad. It was all up to him. Delegation did not come naturally to him. Detectives Kennedy, Black, Connors and Doyle, gathered in the Squad Room for the Monday morning meeting.

1

Rankin had carried on the tradition of the officer before him of addressing squad members by their surnames. To a man, they were happy with Rankin's appointment.

The Homicide Squad, that Rankin now commanded had the abilities necessary to achieve results. Kennedy was a technical investigator. Black was steadfast and taciturn. He said little, but missed nothing. Connors had a private school education, BA, and a moneyed family, but had chosen the police service over a professional career. Doyle, the new member was a recruit by Rankin from the CIB at Fortitude Valley. Doyle was happy to be promoted to homicide.

***

The call came Tuesday at two pm. Details were scant. Two bodies had been found on a bush track in the far north of the state. They had been there some time. It was believed to be murder. Rankin and one of his team, Black, flew to Cairns on a commercial Viscount plane, arriving at eight pm. They were met at the airport by a police car and taken to the far north Queensland Police Headquarters. Rankin knew Bowen, the local Superintendent. Introductions were made. Hardy, the young local Chief Inspector, would be working with the State Homicide Squad if needed.

Bowen spread out a map on an interview room table. A yellow line drawn on the map commenced at a town called Dimbulah and finished at a town called Mt Carbine, about eighty miles away.

Two ghost towns on the bush track. Kingsborough, a deserted railway fettler's camp, and Mt Mulligan, a deserted coal mining town, were between Dimbulah and Mt Carbine.

Since the coal mines had ceased operating, the road between them was very seldom used and was now a bush track and not maintained.

Stopping for lunch by the roadside, two German tourists had noticed a strong feral smell carried on the breeze. Expecting a dead animal, they were not prepared for the sight that lay before them. When they recovered from the shock, they drove to the nearest police station at Dimbulah to report what they had seen. Young, the Senior Sergeant at Mareeba, the police district headquarters drove with two uniformed constable to where the bodies lay. After inspecting the badly decomposed bodies, they taped off the area immediately surrounding them. They were joined by the local CIB. Police roadblocks now guarded each end of the bush track.

Rankin was given an unmarked police vehicle and they were booked into the best hotel in Cairns – its twenty-four-hour room service meant they were fed and on the road at 6am.

At Mareeba, they were joined by the Chief Detective Robbins and the Senior Sergeant Young. Together they drove to the location of the dead bodies. The forensic van was fifteen minutes in front of them.

The elderly Senior Sergeant told them that the bodies could have remained undetected for years except for the Germans' curiosity and a southerly wind blowing.

He had been a police officer at Mt Mulligan years ago when the mines were working. He stated it was now a deserted town, every house and building had been relocated – only the stumps remained standing like sentries. Mt Mulligan was the scene of the biggest mine explosion in the nation's history in 1921, when seventy-five miners died. Mining had continued for almost forty years until the Tully hydroelectric came on stream and there was no longer a need for its coal. The rail line was torn up and the dirt road neglected. It was now a narrow dirt track. The town's hardy residents were long gone.

They arrived at the murder site and parked up-wind from the smell of the dead bodies.

The forensic team had set up their tent and were well under way with their procedures.

Senior Sergeant Young told them the murder scene had once been the ant-bed tennis court, bare, with no weeds or trees. The inexperienced police photographer had been sick near the scene. Thomas, the local Senior Forensic Officer, emerged from the taped off area. 'Females, mature, no ID or personal effects, all pockets empty. Been dead for months. Back of heads caved in, killed at the site, I believe. Only standout is that both have expensive Doc Martin long boots on.'

Rankin, Black and Robbins entered the taped off area. It was a sickening sight – two lives left to rot in the middle of nowhere. Rankin struggled to overcome nausea. Robbins was retching. Black, ever the stoic, was unmoved.

The bodies were rotten, almost skeletons. Only shreds of clothes were barely clinging to bones and rotted flesh. The women wore long boots over what had once been jeans. The faces were missing, probably eaten by wild

4

pigs or dingos, and birds, probably crows, had picked their eyes out. Ants, flies, and other insects were all over the bodies. They were on their backs, ten feet apart. The smell of decayed flesh was overpowering. This was a first sickening sight for Rankin since the exhuming of the murdered Cobb girl last year.

Forensic was ready to bag the bodies for the long trip back to the Cairns' morgue.

Rankin stared at the murder scene, looking for the secrets it might reveal.

There had been rain and storms in the area that had contaminated the site. He knew the killer, or killers, could have had a lot of blood on their clothing. Also, the victims must have had personal effects stripped from them. The killer, or killers, would have left the site by one of the two track entrances.

Rankin got a large torch from the boot of the police car. He and Black went into the mine tunnel entrance, which was below a small cliff.

Fifty yards into the tunnel, they were met by a colony of bats. They both felt uneasy in the musty, foul-smelling tunnels. Rankin considered the killer could have dumped evidence in the tunnels, but discounted that idea as the tunnels quickly became narrow.

He asked the Senior Sergeant where the town had got its water from and he told him there was a natural dam above the mines. The access to it was by a steep path from the right side. Rankin and Black climbed to the rock dam. The remains of a pumping station stood there.

The scene told them there was nothing to be gained there. They returned to the vehicle, ordered the bodies bagged and told Thomas that Mullins, the state senior coroner, would be carrying out the autopsies. They had nothing concrete to start with until the forensic report was completed. Rankin sat thinking in the front seat. *Who were they? Who had killed them? Why were they murdered? How did they get here? If by car, where was the vehicle? Why were they killed at the clear site?*

***

Back at the Mareeba police station, he made a phone call to Commissioner Wirth, bringing him up date and stated he required the State Senior Forensic Officer Mullins to do forensic examination of the women's bodies. The request was expedited by the Commissioner. Press and TV were at the station gate asking questions, as they knew something big had happened.

Rankin gave the press a brief summary of what was unfolding, as he needed their help. The murder would be on TV tonight and in the papers tomorrow with an appeal for information. He believed the boots were important and wanted them highlighted.

He made a quick telephone call to a seller in Brisbane, who informed him that the inner sole of all the boots had initials stamped on them. These markings revealed the year of manufacture. He told Rankin the market for them was limited in Australia as they were very expensive.

A quick call to Thomas retrieved the information on their boots and it was passed on to the dealer.

He told Rankin they would have been made last year. Rankin thanked him. He rang the missing person's departments. There was no match for the women. He also established there was no hire car missing from any hire car firms in the north.

An incident board was set up at Mareeba police headquarters. It asked the questions they needed answers to: Who were the victims? Unknown. Who killed them? Unknown. Why killed? Unknown. Where killed? Known. How killed? Known. When killed? Months ago.

Mullins, with two assistants, would be in Cairns tomorrow. Bookings were made for Rankin and Black at a local hotel with a special request for a private telephone in Rankin's room.

The press were in Mareeba in large numbers now. TV cameras were busy filming and newspaper reporters were jostling at the gate of the police station asking a flurry of questions. Rankin now ignored them, as did Black, but they knew by the questions being asked that someone had been talking to the reporters about the case. Attempts by the press to go to the murder scene were stopped by police at the bush track entrances. Tonight, another police appeal for assistance would be on TV, and it would be in the papers tomorrow and in the weekend editions.

The first question Rankins wanted answered was the identity of the women. The second: what they were doing at Mt Mulligan? He knew that the women must have arrived through one of the bush tracks entrances. But how? Did the killer take them there?

Police were manning phones as information came in from the public. All had to be followed up. But they went nowhere. Rankin did not want to tie up police except for phones ins and following up leads, until he knew who the women were. .

Senior Forensic Officer Mullins rang next day, advising that the cause of death was a severe blow by a blunt instrument to the back of the head of one woman and many blows to the back of the head to the other. The weapon was possibly a small axe or tomahawk. The women were in their early twenties, had no ID, watches, or money on them. Clothes were cheap jeans and shirts. The only things of significance were the good quality, Doc Martin, long boots. What remained of their clothing had no laundry marks. One of the women had broken her left arm when she was a child; the other had a small depression on her forehead.

The newspapers featured the murders on the front pages. TV stations ran them as lead stories. They contained a police plea for any information that would assist them. The Doc Martins boots were highlighted. All police stations in the area were busy taking calls and recording information. Their officers were following leads from the phone calls. It was difficult to progress the investigation without identification or photos.

Both Thomas and Mullins agreed both the victims were killed at the murder site – approximately three months ago, in Mullin's opinion. That would be in December last year.

Next morning, following an early breakfast at their hotel, Rankin and Black returned to Mareeba police headquarters to be updated on the night shifts' inquiries. A nationwide investigation of missing persons revealed no matchup with the murdered women.

Nothing changed over the weekend. By Monday, the police investigation had revealed nothing of importance. The operation was running down as police were being withdrawn.

Rankin was puzzled that there was no record of missing persons to match the victims. Despite a TV and newspaper appeal for information, nothing valuable had come in the seven days since he took over the inquiry.

Then a waitress at a Cairn's café rang the local police station and said that two young women had been at the café where she worked about three months ago with two young men. She told police the women were pommies. She wouldn't have remembered them except the two girls wore Doc Martin boots, which she was saving to buy. She said that they got into a red open-top car with two good-looking young men. She noticed the car, which was really something, as was the driver.

Hardy, the senior detective at Cairns located a vehicle as described by the girl and told Rankin they were holding two men at his station. They were brothers, Karl and Lucas Holzimer. They had lived in the Cairns area for years, but were not known to the police. Under questioning, the Holzimer brothers admitted that a couple of months ago they had given two women hitchhikers a lift from Tully to Cairns, but they parted with them after a meal at a café and a trip to the northern beaches.

The women were English journalists. Their names were Beth and Joanne. They were doing features on Australian culture and ghost towns. The Holzimer brothers had suggested an overnight stay and a tour of the tablelands next day, but the women were not interested. They thought they were probably lesbians.

The men were engine drivers at the local sugar mill. They had finished work when the cane season was over, but stayed in the mill barracks in the off season. They were coming back from a week on an island off Mackay when they picked up the hitchhikers. Both women had large backpacks, brief cases, and diaries. They wore long boots, as they were fearful of snakes.

Requestioned by Rankin, they stuck to their story. Rankin thought the murdered women could be the hitchhikers they had picked up. The young men said they had considered the murdered women the press was writing about could have been the hitchhikers, but thought they would only have grief if they reported it. Rankin thought if the victims were hitchhikers that explained why there was no car to be found. But the question of how they got to isolated Mt Mulligan remained.

Rankin said to Black, 'Looks like Beth and Joanne could be our victims, but things are not always as they appear to be. We need the ID of the girls confirmed.'

Every policeman available was now checking all hotels and accommodation places in Cairns. A police officer found that they had stayed at a hotel on what was called the Barbary Coast, a low rent area around the wharves in Cairns. Six hotels dotted the strip opposite the Cairns wharves.

These were the preferred drinking hole of seamen from different nations, wharfies, and some locals. The area had a reputation for brawls. The publican at the one where the women had stayed was an ex-policeman. He had taken details from them, together with their passport details. He said a lot of prostitutes worked the area, but very few females stopped at his hotel. Rankin and Black interviewed him at his office. The names of the women were Elizabeth Margaret Burke and Joanne Alice Hardgrave. He said they had stayed two nights and interviewed seaman and wharfies. The women had told him they were interested in this country's lifestyle, different cultures, and old deserted towns that were a shell of what they once were. They told him they had taken a trip to the hippy community at Kuranda, then west to a number of ghost towns that were once thriving communities. They had stayed with him from the tenth of December last year and left on the twelfth. Rankin asked the publican if the women had wallets. He was told they both had wraparound wallets with their details, passports, and family photos in them.

The Holzimer brothers, owners of the red tourer, remained in the cells at the Cairn's police headquarters while the Kuranda police checked to confirm that the women had visited the commune there. Those enquiries established that they had spent a day there. Rankin asked the car owners where they were the day the women left Kuranda. A cane farmer verified that they spent the week with him planting next season's crop.

Releasing the brothers, Rankin told them they were free to go.

However, all goodwill had vanished from the brothers. As they departed the interview room, Karl said to the detectives, 'We are going to report you for holding us here overnight.'

Rankin replied, 'If you want to play hard, you will be arrested for withholding vital information in a murder case and will face the court tomorrow.'

'Point taken,' said Karl. They swaggered out of the police station.

With something now to work on, the Immigration Department was requested to provide the women's time of entry into Australia. Three days later, the homicide detectives now knew that the women had arrived by air in Australia in September, six months ago. Rankin now believed he knew who the victims were, but asked the Police Commissioner to inform Scotland Yard and ask them to confirm their identity before releasing details to the press. Scotland Yard contacted the women's parents and established that Beth had broken her right arm as a child and that Joanne had a depression in her forehead, the result of a bad fall from a pushbike.

The parents were devastated. The women had sent Christmas cards home and said they would be home by Easter next year.

Rankin had to mark time for a week, awaiting this information and the clear photos he wanted of the victims. With fifty clear copies of the English photos, he could now launch a major investigation. It was over three weeks since the bodies were found. Now the English press was demanding answers.

By now, all members of the State Homicide Squad had joined Rankin and Black on the investigation. It was a major inquiry and centred on the Atherton Tablelands. Police at last had something to go on.

A publican at Herberton contacted police and told them that two women, who could the victims, had stayed the night at his hotel. Rankin and Black went to his hotel and established it was the missing women. They had been seen writing notes from interviews with locals and taking pictures. They had left next day and said they were going to Chillagoe. The publican said it was the local Atherton race day, the day they had left. He had not tied the women to the murders until he saw the photos in the local paper. They had paid cash and he had not entered them in the hotel register.

Rankin sent Kennedy and Doyle to Chillagoe to interview the publican there, as the victims could have stayed there, and to talk to the locals. Late that afternoon, Kennedy reported that two women had come to Chillagoe in what a resident said was a flash car. It had delivered them there and left, and then had picked them up late afternoon. The local was English and remembered them because they were from her homeland. She had spent time with them and introduced them to her friends. The women asked a lot of questions about the town and its history and took photos.

Kennedy with Doyle had then gone to the only pub in the area to speak to the publican. The publican and his wife looked at the photos and had to think back three months. They said it was just before Christmas when two young men arrived at the hotel.

The publican remembered them. The men had played wall quoits and pool with his locals. They drank steadily and were no trouble. They had left late in the afternoon in a black Humber Hawk sedan, and returned with the two women in the photo. They had a few drinks and left. The women were poms. He did not notice which way they were travelling.

When asked why he had not informed police of this, he stated that he barely remembered them until questioned. He knew about the murders, but had not connected them. He remembered the Humber Hawk sedan, as he was interested in buying one and questioned the owners about its performance.

Everything pointed to the women being with the men in the Humber Hawk. Rankin told Robbins to put out an alert for all Humber Hawk vehicles owners in the area, especially owned by young men.

Next morning, Robbins had the details Rankin wanted. A Humber Hawk sedan was owned by two timber cutters now working in the rainforest areas of the Tablelands and living at a local hotel there. Robbins stated the men, Ben and Neville Baxter had been in the area for over a year had no police form. Their known habits were drinking, women, and occasionally punting. They had a very dangerous, highly paid occupation and lived on the edge. Rankin rang the publican, identified himself, and asked the whereabouts of the brothers. The publican asked why he wanted it. Rankin told him they could help his murder investigation into the women found murdered at Mt Mulligan. They could have seen something of importance and not realised it.

He was informed by the publican that the two brothers, Ben and Neville Baxter, stayed with him and were cutting timber in the rainforest adjoining the hotel. They were quiet and never gave any trouble.

They had a black Humber Hawk, and an old Dodge ute they used for work. They had been with him on and off for six months. Rankin thanked him and established that the men were working that day. He was told they usually got home around five pm.

At five, Rankin and Black were at the hotel waiting to interview the two men. The men arrived thirty minutes later in a white Dodge utility and parked it at the rear of the hotel beside a black Humber Hawk, four door sedan. A large caravan was parked behind the vehicles.

Rankin and Black approached the timber cutters. After asking them to sit at a table in the hotel dining room, the questioning commenced.

Ben Baxter freely admitted they had twice picked up the two hitchhikers.

The first time, it had been too wet to work. They had driven to Atherton to buy two saw files. Next morning, they had driven to Innisfail, returning on the following day. On the way to Innisfail, they gave two pommie women a lift to Herberton. They came back for the local races at Atherton. The two women were outside a service station hitching a lift. They stopped and the women recognised them. They were trying to get to Chillagoe. The women had large backpacks, which they again loaded into their sedan. As they had nothing really back-able at the races, they decided to drive the girls to Chillagoe.

They dropped the girls off then spent the rest of the day at the pub. They picked the girls up late in the afternoon, went to the pub, and had a round of drinks. The women had wanted to go to Mt Mulligan, but they told them it would be difficult to get there hitchhiking, as there

15

would be little traffic, if any, on the road there. They said they would look at their options tomorrow. Cooktown interested them and Atherton was a good place to leave from. They came to a servo in Atherton, had tea with the Baxters, and left about them around ten pm. Beth had left them for a short time to arrange accommodation for the night. The Baxters returned to their hotel had a few beers and went to bed.

Rankin heard them out and then said, 'What were the women doing at Chillagoe?'

Ben said, 'Research on old ghost towns. Mt Mulligan was next on their list, then Cooktown. We were committed to help load a timber truck next afternoon and did, otherwise we would have taken them there. They were good company. We were back in the rainforest early next morning as it was dry enough to work. We felled trees until the log carrier arrived.'

Rankin asked, 'Why did you go to Innisfail?'

Ben replied, 'We have girlfriends there and stopped with them overnight at the Royal Hotel.'

After noting the details of the timber truck driver, Rankin continued, 'You were not surprised to see us?'

Ben replied, 'We realised the bodies found at Mt Mulligan could be the women we were with, decided to say nothing as we were liable to be suspects and that could only bring us trouble.'

Rankin said, 'You withheld vital information.'

'No,' said Neville, 'we only assumed the murdered women were the ones we knew.'

Rankin continued, 'What time did you get back here that night?'

Ben said, 'About ten-fifteen, just on closing time. We had a couple of beers on our tab and went to bed.'

The publican was able to confirm that the brothers had added two beers each to their tab that night about closing time.

Rankin and Black inspected the Humber Hawk sedan. It was clean inside and out. In the boot, there was a folded tent, an Engle fridge, gas bottle, a small stove, a box of cooking utensils, sleeping bags, beach towels, and rubbish bags.

Then they inspected the tray of the Dodge ute, which had a cross cut saw, two axes, wedges, lights, three foot boards, brush hook, steel brand, and a tomahawk. Ben said all trees they felled had to have the butt branded and the back of the tomahawk was perfect for it. It was also used to cut kindling if they wanted a fire when camping. Ben told them they always brought their work gear home, as there were always thieves around.

Rankin asked about the caravan and Ben said, 'That's usually our home, but our present boss pays our board at the hotel and the rooms are more comfortable.'

There was an iron fireplace with a tank above it behind the hotel. Rankin asked its purpose and was informed it was called a Donkey. The fire supplied heat to the tank above it, which supplied hot water to the hotel.

Rankin inspected it to find that it had a grated area with a log burning above it. It had a damper to regulate the fire. He tested the water in the hotel laundry and it was hot.

Back at Mareeba, the detectives soon established where the women had stayed for the night. The hotel was in the centre of the street. The publican was helpful. He stated that the women had slept on low stretchers on the veranda as he was booked out on race day. They had left early the following morning. The hotel cook had given them a six o'clock breakfast then went to the newsagency. They were at the front of the hotel when she left, but gone when she returned to her kitchen fifteen minutes later.

The timber hauler confirmed the Baxter's statement about loading the truck. In passing, he said the brothers must have started early as they had three big trees on the ground for the next load when he got there. He considered they probably were going away for a few days and wanted logs on the ground.

***

Rankin gathered his team and Robbins around the white board in the incident room. The question of who the victims were was answered. Where killed was answered. How killed was answered. But why and who killed them were unanswered. The murder victims were at the diner there at around ten the day of the local races, if the Baxter's were to be believed. But Rankin needed proof. He thought they could have arranged with someone at the servo to be taken to Mt Mulligan.

Rankin returned to the hotel where the victims had stayed. The publican said the two women had arrived at his hotel about ten-thirty the night of the races. Asked if the women had been in the bar, the publican was nervous as ten pm closing was the law, but when informed that they were not interested in trading out of hours, the publican became talkative. The girls had a few drinks before going to their beds on the upstairs veranda. A few drinkers had tried to join them, but had been rebuffed. When they left the bar, three men had followed them out and talked to them at the foot of the stairs.

The publican said he knew one of the men who were talking to the girls at the stairs. His bar was packed with strangers from the races as well as locals. After getting the name and known details of the local, Rankin and Black interviewed him. He said he and his mates were going to an all-night party and asked the girls to join them. When they declined the offer, he left them. The three had watertight alibies for next morning – hung over and sleeping it off at their mate's home.

After reconsidering the hotel cook's statement, Rankin thought the Baxter brothers appeared to be clear of any suspicion that they could have murdered them, because of the time frame when they left Chillagoe and time they arrived home. If their time with the Baxter's ended at around ten pm, the women could have arranged to go to Mt Mulligan with someone they met later that evening, at either the servo, or the hotel.

Again, Rankin revisited the hotel cook. The hotel was in the centre of the block and Rankin established that the women were not carrying backpacks when they waited outside the hotel. They were waiting for someone, he reasoned.

He and his men obtained a list of all employees working in the servo the night of the races and interviewed the cook who was working that night with four waitresses. She said she and the assistant cook were too busy to notice anything as the local and race crowd had filled the dining room. The detectives located the assistant cook and four waitresses working that night. None had any useful information. They said they had been very busy the night of the races.

Police interviewed local people who had been at the hotel that night, but drinking made memories vague.

The police search had spread north, as the Baxters had indicated the women were going to bypass Mt Mulligan and go to Cooktown. They thought they might have gone north, then been offered transport to Mt Mulligan from Mt Carbine, but a large police investigation there had revealed nothing.

Now the search centred around Atherton and the Dimbulah area – the entrance to the Mt Mulligan road.

The papers and TV wanted results as the bodies had been discovered almost a month ago. The English press had arrived in swarms outside the Mareeba police station. They had been relentless in their demands and had been starting to question Rankin's ability to handle the job – hinting that his quick promotion to department head was an error of judgement.

Outwardly, Rankin was unruffled, inwardly, he was mentally, and physical tired, and was sleeping badly.

The Commissioner was under pressure for a result, but he knew what Rankin had accomplished since the discovery of the bodies. Rankin called his team, plus Robbins, to a meeting at nine o'clock next morning – twenty-eight days after the bodies were discovered.

At the meeting, he noted the relevant facts of the case to date. He then talked about how they were last seen outside the hotel they had stayed at on the day of the races, almost four month ago. He believed someone had agreed to take them to where they were murdered. That explained why they remained outside the hotel. They were waiting for someone to pick them up.

WHO, he wrote in big letters on the board. What happened at Mt Mulligan? Where were the backpacks, brief case, notes, clothing wallets, money?

He said the responses from the papers and TV police appeal for assistance resulted in many leads that went nowhere. The press were losing interest in the case. The search for the killer or killers had got nowhere.

With nothing further to go on, Rankin sent Kennedy, Black, and Connors back to Brisbane where they had a backlog of work to be done. Doyle stayed with him. Rankin studied the incident board, which was now crowded with information that had been crossed out as things were eliminated, but the important *why* and *who* were still unanswered. The solid facts were the Baxter brothers' statement of where the women had been and intended to go and the hotel cook's statement of where they were last seen.

He went through what they knew of the killer or killers of the women. There would have been a lot of blood shed around the bodies and the murderer or murderers would have been covered in it.

Going back to basics, he said it was indisputable where the women were last seen, and what they were doing before they vanished was highly relevant. Was this case to become an unsolved murder like the murder of the woman at Southport last year? He believed he knew who her murderers were, but had no evidence to prove it. He had no one in the frame for this one, and no real suspects.

Rankin, Doyle, and Robbins went through all reports looking for anything of interest, but CIB and uniform had been very thorough in their investigations.

Robbins said, 'Senior Sergeant Young told me he was surprised at the Baxters early start the morning after their big day with the women. They must have been hung over, but did not sleep in, as you would expect. They had trees on the ground early and were only required to load a truck at two pm. Robbins said his father had been a timber cutter. It was a very dangerous occupation where split second decisions were often needed. Not a job for hung-over men. But their alibi was iron clad.

They went on reading reports, but Rankin, who had mulled over what Robbins said, started to analyse a theory. He shared it with his team. 'The timber hauler had said they were probably going away for a few days. Whoever killed the women had to think fast, destroy all identity, and hope the bodies were not found in the near future. Then clean themselves up and drive out of there carrying the backpacks and records.

A Baxter brother could have picked the women up at the pub and then taken them to Mt Mulligan, gone back to work, and loaded the timber truck, and then returned to collect the women after they loaded the truck. This gave the victims a lot of unhurried time at Mt Mulligan.'

But Rankin knew it was all theory and no facts. They had no eye witness or motive and there were many vehicles in town that morning. Rankin realised it was a wild theory, but it was the best he had. The trip to Mt Mulligan from the Baxter's hotel and back would have taken under three hours. The Donkey fireplace would have been the way to burn and destroy all papers, wallets, the briefcase, and their contents. The backpacks could have been buried. Their bloody clothes could have been bagged in a rubbish bag and then put through the pub washing machine. Rankin realised he was going out on a limb and could make a complete fool of himself challenging a water tight alibi.

Rankin rang Thomas, the forensic officer in Cairns, and asked him to bring an assistant to join him tomorrow afternoon at Mareeba. At five pm, Rankin, Doyle, Robbins, Thomas, and his assistant were at the brothers' pub. Rankin told the publican, 'We have work to do. Please don't interfere.' The Baxter brothers arrived home and Rankin said, 'We want to search your rooms.'

Ben replied, 'Have you got a search warrant?'

Rankin said, 'I can soon get one.'

Ben said, 'One room at a time and we must be there.'

They searched Neville's room and found nothing of interest. He was evidently a reader of novels, including crime stories.

Ben's room yielded nothing except the fact that he also read books including crime novels but many people read them. Thomas minutely examined the Humber Hawk, as his assistant combed the ashes from the Donkey, which were used to fill holes in the yard. Thomas found no blood in the Humber Hawk. The finger prints of the women in the vehicle were expected and the tomahawk was clean. Thomas disconnected the elbow of the sink and scanned for blood, and also checked where the washing machine water ran out on the lawn, but found nothing. Thomas's assistant had found in the Donkey fireplace a book spine, a long zipper, and evidence of plastic being burnt there, but the publican told Rankin all things that would burn went into the Donkey. There was no garbage collection here. All rubbish that would not burn had to be binned and taken to the council dump. Rankin, his team, Thomas and his assistant had come up with nothing. They left the hotel and the Baxter brothers with no apology.

Rankin and his team returned to Mareeba, Thomas and his assistant to Cairns.

Something was nagging at Rankin, but he could not put his finger on it. He sat in his hotel room that night after Doyle and Robbins had gone to the bar. Regardless of the facts, he had been so wrong about the Baxters. But they were two of the last people to be with the girls, and still suspects as far as he was concerned.

Then it hit him, he had assumed the Humber Hawk would have been the vehicle used, but what about the Dodge ute. That made sense. He rang Thomas and asked him with his assistant to join him tomorrow at Mareeba. Rankin had a bad night's sleep. He could be clutching at straws.

Thomas joined Rankin, Doyle, and Robbins at nine the next morning. They drove to where the Baxters were working. The ute was at the rainforest entrance. It was unlocked and Thomas started to dust its inside. After a short time, he said, 'The women were in this vehicle, but there's no sign of blood.' After a short trip back to Mareeba, Rankin asked the Sergeant to bring the brothers to the police station.

Two constables left in a police car. An hour later, the Baxters were at the station. One constable said, 'They were very argumentative, but did not resist us. They wanted to complete felling a tree and take their work gear home to their hotel. They were surprised at the fingerprint dust in the ute.' The brothers were taken to separate interview rooms.

'What now?' said Robbins.

Rankin said, 'We will question the brothers separately. Now let's understand the ground rules. I ask the questions and neither of you speak unless I ask you to.' They went to the interview room where Neville had been directed. The room had a table and four chairs, two each side of it. Neville sat on one side of the table with Doyle, Rankin, and Robbins opposite him.

Rankin turned on a tape recorder and with no preamble said, 'Truth time, Neville, no more lies.'

Neville said, 'I have nothing to say.'

Rankin nodded. 'This is only an informal talk, which you were good enough to come to the station for.'

Neville said, 'We were dragged here.'

Rankin repeated, 'Truth time now, Neville, I am sick of your lies.'

Neville shook his head. 'I have nothing to say.'

Rankin asked the constables to take Neville to a holding cell and to bring Ben to the interview room. They resumed the seating arrangements. Rankin again turned on the recorder and opened with, 'Truth time, Ben, no more lies.'

Ben said, 'I will be glad to tell it. Neville and I have had enough. I told him to say nothing and let me explain what happened. On the way back with them from Chillagoe on the Saturday they asked us to take them to Mt Mulligan and then to Cooktown. They offered a fee for service, but they insisted on a first class hotel. They said they were not available in the back seat of cars. We arranged to meet them next morning at the pub where they were staying and take them to Mt Mulligan. Neville did this in our work vehicle, after dropping me off to work. He left them at a clear space with our Engle cooled down, with soft drink and food in it and two gallons of water in a plastic container. He came home and went to work with me. As we would be away for a day or two, we had to have another load cut by next weekend.

'We loaded the log carrier, went home to our pub, cleaned up, got dressed, and went in the Humber to join them at Mt Mulligan. I went to a public phone and booked us in for the night at Hydes, the best hotel in Cairns, then went to collect the women. What greeted us was a nightmare. Both Betty and Joanne were dead. Their heads were caved in and they were covered in blood. All our gear was gone, including the water container.

'We got out of there and left by the other track exit. We were shocked and didn't know what to do. We drove to Innisfail and then to Etta Bay, rigged the tent and sat at the beach. We were still awake when the sun came up. We didn't know what to do. Everything would point to us as the people who had killed them if we told the police. We decided to do nothing.

'Next day, we replaced our Engle at Innisfail, hired a boat, went fishing, and tried to put everything behind us. We went back to work. After the months went by, we hoped they would not be found for years. But when the bodies were found, we knew the police would become aware of our contact with the murdered women, but all known contact would cease at the servo. That's it.'

Rankin said, 'Where did you buy the missing Engle?'

'Innisfail, where I bought the Humber Hawk.'

'Have you got a number for the Engle?' Rankin asked,

Ben said, 'All our papers are in a drawer in my hotel room, including the Innisfail receipts for the gear we replaced.'

Doyle was sent to get them.

Rankin said, 'That's all for now, but you and your brother are guilty of a number of crimes, including not reporting a murder, and withholding vital information in a murder inquiry.'

Ben was taken to another cell. Rankin replayed Ben's original statement and noted the salient points. They could have been the last to see the victims alive. They had not reported this or the theft of their Engle; both would have had a big bearing on the investigation. He contacted all Engle dealers in the north, issuing an alert on the stolen one, and on the battery and electric cables. He believed they were still in the Humber Hawk and would have to be replaced.

Rankin had both the brothers' vehicles brought to the Mareeba police yard; the two Engle fridge cables were in the Humber Hawk.

He rang Hydes Hotel in Cairns and stated who he was. Ben's statement regarding the booking was confirmed. He then rang the Etta Bay camp manager and identified himself. He told her what he wanted and she said that would take time to verify, but she would ring him back. Rankin, Doyle, and Robbins waited for her call.

Not waiting for her call, Rankin said, 'We have enough to hold them, between finding murdered bodies and not reporting it, and impeding a murder investigation.'

He had them brought to the interview room, read them their rights and formally arrested them. He advised the station sergeant to get them solicitors. They had their belts and shoe laces removed, and pockets emptied. Santo, the solicitor appointed to represent Ben, arrived and interviewed him in his cell, as did Neville's solicitor, Lewis.

The park manager rang back. She reported that a Ben Baxter and his brother Neville had been there on the dates given. They and had been there before. They had hired a boat from her for the two days they were there, which they usually did. What time they arrived she didn't know. The camping area was always open and many people arrived and set up camp after she closed the office and settled with her next morning.

Doyle and Robbins had established that the brothers had bought an Engle fridge at Innisfail on Monday the seventeenth of December – the day after the women were last seen. He rang Commissioner Wirth, informing him that a new inquiry was now underway, and two suspects were in custody on charges related to the murders. The arrest of the brothers had renewed press interest in the case and they were gathering outside the police station.

A police bulletin had gone out to all Engle dealers, second hand dealers, and camp outfitters with the stolen Engle's number. Rankin believed it could be sold. Even though the Engle would have to have electric cables bought for it, it was worth money, even second hand. The brothers fronted the Magistrates Court and were held over on the charges laid.

Rankin knew the killer or killers could have left the scene clean of blood, but would have had to know where the dam was, and know the track to it.

Local knowledge, he thought, *or information given.* If the brothers were telling the truth, someone had killed the women between when they left them and when they came back to pick them up. About nine hours. The motive could have been robbery, but why kill them? Also, they were found where Ben Baxter said they left them. That could mean they had come back there for lunch. If that was the case, they could have been killed around midday.

Rankin was deep in thought. He asked the Senior Sergeant Young about locals who could have been in the area at any time. Young said that roo shooters sometimes worked the area, but very seldom. He knew them all and they had been questioned, and their utes inspected during the police operation early in the original investigation.

He set up a fresh incident white board. He wrote the murdered women's names on the incident board and wrote; Date murdered; known. Where murdered; known.

Why murdered; unknown. Murderer or Murderers; unknown. Suspects: Baxter brothers, but they have a plausible explanation for all their actions. There had been no response yet about the stated stolen property of the Baxter's.

Rankin played the recording of both brothers' statements. Neville's brief and Ben's long. Doyle said, 'Their agreement was for Ben to do all the talking and Neville to remain silent. The boat hire is interesting. They could have dumped all the missing gear out at sea – the backpacks and the women's diary and notes.'

'No,' said Rankin, 'Any paperwork would have gone through the hotel Donkey fire, if the Baxters are guilty.'

Robbins said, 'The women's fingerprints in the Dodge were not cleaned and removed.'

'Helps their case, a botched attempt to clean them off would be suspicious and really in our favour.' Doyle and Robbins were silent.

Rankin said, 'Tomorrow, Doyle will go to Etta Bay with Thomas, the Cairns' forensic head, examine the boat for any blood samples and gather all information on the Baxters' stay there in December. Robbins and another police officer will get all clothing and footwear from the hotel where they stayed, bag it, and have it sent to Thomas.'

***

Doyle rang him, late that afternoon and said Thomas had turned up nothing on the boat. Doyle had questioned the manager at Etta Bay and the Baxters had often gone night fishing in the hire boat. The boat was a twenty-two foot motorised vessel.

Rankin thought, *What if the Baxters had not changed at their hotel and had met the women wearing their work clothes*. That made it a new ball game. Baxter's clothing from the hotel had been sent to Thomas, but all tests were negative. No blood in the vehicle, clothes, or boat. The case against the Baxters was very weak, but Rankin saw another way of proving if the Baxters were guilty or innocent. If they had met the women wearing their work clothes, they would have had their work boots on. Their boot laces had been removed at the station and they were now wearing prison garb and lace less boots. They boots were sent to Thomas.

Rankin met with Doyle and Robbins next morning and said, 'The brothers could have met the women straight after loading the logs on the timber truck. They would change later to casual clothing. Something went wrong at the reunion with the women at Mt Mulligan. Both women were killed. Ben has a sharp brain and used it. He has covered all bases.'

Thomas rang that afternoon from the lab stating that there was evidence of feint blood stains matching both women on Ben's boot lace holes and Joanne's blood on Neville's boot lace holes. Rankin sat thinking in the incident room. The evidence of the blood was weak but enough for him. He visualised the murder scene with the Baxters in their work clothes.

Beth killed by Ben with one blow to the head. Joanne by both men, and in anger, by the many blows to the head.

Rankin rang Commissioner Wirth and stated that the two suspects would now be charged with murder.

Wirth replied, 'Thank Christ for that, the press has been barking ever since you reopened the inquiry.'

Rankin said, 'They have been outside Mareeba station for days.'

Rankin requested Thomas be in the court for the hearing the next day.

Ben and Neville Baxter were brought to the interview room. Rankin, Doyle, and Robbins sat one side of the table opposite Ben and Neville and there legal aid solicitors. Two constables were outside the door. Rankin turned on the tape recorder, stated, time, date, reason for the interview, and who was present. Rankin asked Ben his full name and date of birth. Ben gave it. Rankin then asked Neville the same questions. He then appeared to relax and said to Ben, 'We have solid evidence that you and your brother murdered the two women at Mt Mulligan.'

'It wasn't us,' said Ben.

Rankin continued, Robbins and Doyle watched. Rankin said, 'I told you, we have positive proof you and your brother are responsible for the women's murders. Do you want to tell us anything about it?'

The duty solicitor Santo said, 'Our clients will deny this.'

Rankin produced the photos of the women taken by the police photographer and handled them to the brothers saying, 'Two young women with their whole life in front of them. Look how they wound up.' Ben shuddered at the graphic photos and Neville looked away. His solicitor, who was white-faced said, 'That was out of order, Chief Inspector.'

Rankin ignored him and said, 'Forensic evidence proves the murders were committed at Mt Mulligan and you, Ben, have both victims' blood in your boot lace holes, your brother has one of the victim's blood in his boot lace holes. The ashes of the Donkey contain evidence of what appears to be the remains of a zip from a briefcase and the metal spine of a notebook.'

'Enough of this questioning – our clients have denied the charges,' said the Santo. Rankin stated the time the interview finished and turned off the recorder. The brothers looked ashen-faced, as were the duty solicitors. The after-death photos were ugly. Ben and Neville were taken back to their cells, and the detectives conferred. Doyle said, 'The accused had a reaction when you showed them the photos.'

Robbins said, 'So did the solicitors … and me.

Rankin let the brothers consider their position hoping for a confession. After fifteen minutes, he had both brothers brought back to the interview room with their solicitors. They had nothing to say and he formally charged them with the murder of the Joanne Burke and Elizabeth Hardgrave, at Mt Mulligan on or about the sixteenth of December last year. Rankin read them their rights.

'On what evidence do you lay these charges?' Neville's solicitor asked.

'As I said before, blood from the murdered women was discovered in the lace holes of both of their boots. That is enough to hold both of them. They will both go down for murder.' Turning to the brothers, Rankin added, 'I am going to dig up that park at the beach at Etta Bay and have divers working off the point where you were seen fishing from your hired boat. The diggers will locate the backpacks and the divers your missing Engle and the women's cameras and personal effects. You are both going down for this, but it's a mystery why you had to kill them.'

Santo, Ben's solicitor, said, 'No evidence of blood was found in their vehicles, is that correct?'

Rankin replied, 'Yes, but we know why. Ben's original statement was not true. They did not change clothes after they loaded the log hauler. They were in their work clothes when they returned to the women at the murder site and they changed there.' The interview was over and the brothers taken back to their cells.

Rankin went back to their room and to the whiteboard. He thought through what action they could have taken after the murders. 'They would have bagged their work clothes in a plastic rubbish bag, then they searched the victims and gathered their notes, diary, watches personal jewellery, and wallets and put them in another bag. He knew both Ben and Neville are crime novel readers and both have a rough idea of how forensic evidence works. All that was left were the backpacks.

'They climbed to the old town dam and washed all blood off them, came back to their vehicle, changed into their casual clothes and left the area. They were in real trouble, but Ben didn't panic. They went to Etta Bay, rigged their tent, went to Innisfail next day, and replaced their alleged stolen Engle and gear.

'I believe they hired the boat and took their alleged stolen Engle and the women's personal effects out to sea in the boat, and scattered everything over a large area. The bagged work clothes went through the laundry at Innisfail, possibly a few times. Their boots were probably washed in the laundry sink, but not thoroughly enough. Now we have a big job to prove our case. It is solid with the blood samples, but they are small and will be severely challenged in court. But we have time to strengthen our case.'

They all went to a café and ordered lunch. The press gathered around the Senior Sergeant who was issuing a press statement. A constable came to the cafe and said Ben Baxter wanted to see the Chief Inspector.

Rankin, Doyle, and Robbins went back to the station. They went back to the interview room. Santo said, 'My client wishes to make a statement.'

The tape recorder was turned on and the usual procedure entered into it. Rankin said, 'You wish to make a statement of your own free will, Mr Benjamin Douglas Baxter?'

Ben said, 'I admit to killing both girls. My brother Neville had no part in this.'

Rankin went to ask a question but Santo said, 'My client has nothing further to say.'

Rankin said, 'I need more than that.' Ben was silent and Rankin said, 'Ben, I don't believe you had any intention of murdering the women, tell me what happened.'

Santo said, 'My client has nothing more to say.'

Rankin was looking at Ben who sighed, slumped, and said, 'It was horrible. I didn't mean to kill them.' Santo went to say something, but Ben waved him aside. 'When we arrived back at Mt Mulligan to pick the women up they said they had changed their minds and would not be going to Cairns tonight, but would deliver their promise after we took them to Cooktown. I said we could stop at Port Douglas on the way, as good accommodation was available there. They agreed to stop there on the way back from Cooktown.

'I knew they were taking us for fools and I would have left them at Mt Mulligan, but Neville didn't want to do that. I said to Neville, "They are a pair of prick teasers, let's go". I started to close the vehicle boot door, having loaded our equipment into the Humber Hawk boot. Beth said, "You can't leave us here", and I said, "Watch me, slut". She attacked me. I grabbed her hands but she sank her teeth into my chest. I picked up the tomahawk that was near the boot door and meant to hit her on the back with the back of it, as she would not let go. But I hit her on the head. She must have had a thin skull, as it caved in.

'Joanna and Neville were frozen in their places. Then Joanna started to scream and run away. I caught up with her and she scratched, bit me, and kneed me where it hurts. I hit her with the back of the tomahawk several times in anger. Neville was trying to stop me.

'She collapsed. I realised both women were dead and started to think clearly. When Neville travelled to Mt Mulligan with the women, they had a history of the place that mentioned a dam above the mines. Neville helped me to search the women, remove all identity and jewellery – bangles, ear rings, and watches, then put them with their wallets, notes, and diary in a heap. Neville washed his hands with water from the container we had left with them. He held a garbage bag open and I put their gear in it. I put the tomahawk in another bag. We stripped off and bagged our bloodstained clothes and boots, then put them in a plastic bag, and the women's effects in another.

'Naked, we climbed to the dam, which the women had pointed out to Neville, wearing our beach thongs, as the going was rough. We went into the dam and washed the blood off. We came back to our sedan, dressed in our casual clothes, loaded their backpacks, and drove out to Mt Carbine and on to Etta Bay. There, we washed our work clothes in the sea and then put them through the laundry at Innisfail a couple of time, after we bought the Engel. Buying new clothes was out as would create suspicion if the police interviewed us about the murders. The rest you know, but I didn't want to kill them. I hit both of them in self-defence.'

'The girl's wallets, ID, and backpacks?' asked Rankin.

'Their ID, wallets, diary notes, and underwear in the backpacks were burnt in the hotel donkey after we came back to the hotel next day. We put a log in the donkey every morning before work and destroyed their effects over a week.

'Their personal things watches earrings, bracelets went overboard at sea, their clothes were bagged and put into charity bins. The backpacks with heavy stones in them also went into the sea. We exposed the camera films, burnt them, and threw their holders and camera overboard. Then we went back to our hotel and back to work.'

Santo said, 'I want it noted that my client cooperated with you and saved the state a lot of money.' Rankin said nothing and left the room with the recorder, he got Ben's statement typed and returned to the room. He gave the typed statement to Ben and said, 'Is this a true record of your statement?'

Ben and Santo read it and Ben said, 'Yes.' Rankin handed him a pen and Santo said, 'You don't have to sign this.' Ben signed it and was taken back to his cell.

Rankin Doyle and Robbins were silent, considering Ben's statement. Rankin said, 'Neat and believable about Neville. But all charges will stand.'

Lewis came to them and said, 'Santo's client takes full responsibility for both murders. My client should not be charged with murder. His charge should be reduced. '

Not in the mood for negotiations, Rankin said tersely, 'Your clients have both been charged with the murders of Joanne Alice Hardgrave and Elizabeth Margaret Burke. They will appear in the Magistrates Court and be bound over.'

The two solicitors left the station. Both ran into a press, hungry for more news. Santo was comfortable with them, but gave vague answers to their questions. Lewis pushed through them and said nothing.

At the Magistrates' court next day, Ben pleaded guilty to the murders but stated it was self-defence and Neville was not guilty of the charge levelled against him. Rankin gave his evidence. There was no questioning by Ben's solicitor, but he made a statement that his client had cooperated willingly with the police. Neville's solicitor stated his client's charge should be downgraded on the evidence of his brother. Rankin said both brothers were guilty as charged. Forensic evidence from Thomas was now damming.

The Magistrate remanded the brothers to the next sitting of the Supreme Court in Cairns and refused bail.

After a handshake and a few words of thanks to Robbins and Young, Rankin and Doyle drove to Cairns. They saw Superintendent Bowen and Chief Detective Hardy, thanked them for their help, and caught the afternoon flight to Brisbane.

It was dark when they landed at Brisbane. Rankin went to his office checked his in-tray, and completed his report to Wirth, which would be delivered by one of his men. It was now late in the evening. Driving home in his private police car Rankin was a happy man. Satisfied and looking forward to a pot of tea and his wife's company. He quickly glanced into the boy's bedroom as he walked into the kitchen. His wife, Rhonda, looked up when he came to the lounge. They were alone. She said, 'Vergil, we have to talk.' This had been brewing all day, he could tell. Sighing, he softly replied, 'Tomorrow, Rhonda, I am very tired.'

'No! Tonight! Vergil, you are obsessed with your job and miss most of what your boys do. You hardly ever see them play sport and miss most school nights when all other parents are there. It was different when you were in the arson squad – you were never away for long. You had time for us then. Look at yourself in the mirror you look a hundred, old and tired, this job will kill you early.'

He stood, taking it all in, and then replied, 'Buildings burnt down can be replaced, but lives cannot. Murder is the most serious crime in civilised society and killers must be brought to justice. That's my job.'

Shaking her head sadly, Rhonda went to bed. Later, when he joined her after showering, he reached for her and she shrugged him off. Rankin realised that eventually his choice would be family or job. The newspapers would now be onside with him. The English papers were silent. He had come through his baptism of fire. He slept well.

He awoke at ten next morning, having slept in. Rhonda and the boys had left for school. He rang Wirth's office and made an appointment for midday.

Wirth was happy with the result and said, 'Good work, Rankin. You did a very good job. Take time off, you have earned it.'

It was Thursday and he decided to take the weekend off and take the family to the coast. He enjoyed the break, as did his family.

When be reached for Rhonda in bed Sunday night, she came to him willingly.

CHAPTER 2

SUSPECT WILLIAMS

Rankin was at his office Monday morning. He went through the reports on the murders that his men were now working on. These murders were motivated by family affairs, jealousy, hatred, alcohol, or drugs and were mundane and easily cleared up by his homicide team or the CIB.

His phone rang. The desk sergeant said, 'A retired CIB detective wants to talk to you.' Rankin replied, 'Send him through.'

The retired detective introduced himself as Ivan Collins. The gaunt, miserable, pinched-faced man in his sixty's extended his hand across the desk. Getting straight to the point, he said he wanted to talk about four murders. The common factor in these murders was a woman whom Collins believed was responsible, but she was never charged. Sceptically, Rankin asked him if the Homicide Squad had been involved. After a heavy sigh, Collins replied, 'Yes, but they got nowhere.'

Rankin said, 'It would be in the files. I will read it.'

Collins said, 'The files will only be reports that go nowhere. I know she is guilty. Maybe you can bring her to justice. I have followed the cases you were involved with under Findlay, your old chief, and latest murder you solved. You think outside the circle, which is why I believe you can bring her before the court.'

Not persuaded, Rankin said he would look at the files. He took Collins number and said he would get back to him.

The first of the case files was ordered from archives.

His former boss, Findlay, then a Detective Sergeant, had worked on the inquiries. Intrigued, Rankin contacted Findlay. He was still on leave, but agreed to meet him at the bistro across the lane from police headquarters.

**

It was good to see Findlay again. Seated in a quiet corner, Rankin told Findlay about the Collins claims and sat back to watch his response. He let out a long breath and finally said, 'Yes, I worked on the cases involved. Collins has a bee in his bonnet about a woman, a real looker, named Elaine Jayne Williams – her maiden name by the way. To give you some background – she was born in one of the Balkan states, arrived as a refugee orphan, and adopted by a well-off family. She now speaks good English, received a degree from a New South Wales University in graphic design, and quickly found employment in Sydney, where she met and married her husband. She claimed she changed her birth name to Williams as no one could pronounce her original name.

'She married an older man, Arthur Davies. He had no children and lived with his spinster sister in a home in Woollahra, Sydney. Davies had extensive interests in the poker machine distribution business in New South Wales. Those machines were banned in Queensland at the time. They relocated to Brisbane when Elaine accepted a job there.

'According to Elaine, Davies believed poker machines could legally operate on cruise ships once they sailed beyond the three mile limit, into international waters. To test the feasibility of his concept, Davies joined a two week boat cruise of the islands off Australia.

When the ship docked on its return in Brisbane, it became apparent that Davies was missing. Initially, the crew conducted a search of the entire ship, but without success. CIB were then called in by the ship owners. They were concerned about the image of the cruise company and requested the least inconvenience to the crew, and most importantly, the passengers.

'All passengers and crew on the cruise ship were questioned by CIB. It seemed no passenger remembered Davies. CIB prepared a file for the Coroner who subsequently found that it was more than likely Davies had drowned at sea. The cruise company expressed its sadness, and reassured the public that its ships and their passengers were safe. Sometimes mysterious things happened at sea, they said.

'Life went on for Collins, myself, CIB and Elaine. As Davies' body was never found, Elaine had to wait seven years to receive the proceeds of a life insurance policy purchased by Davies on his life, soon after the marriage. That insurance payment put her under suspicion, but she had no case to answer, as his body was never found.

Elaine continued to work in Brisbane. Eventually, she was granted a divorce from her missing husband and married a real estate agent of limited finances. They lived in a rented unit on the Gold Coast. She was the main provider.

Whilst she was absent on a business trip to Sydney, six months after she married him, her second husband, the salesman, died of a heart attack. He suffered from high blood pressure and took tablets for it and Viagra to offset its effects on his sex life. The cause of death was attributed to the tablet mix. Elaine Williams had no financial gain from his death and investigations found no other man in her life. Coincidence? Maybe. Husband number 2, dead.

'Life continued for Elaine; she returned to Brisbane, and continued to work. At a Brisbane Exhibition Show Week cocktail party the following year, she met a retired grazier who lived in Brisbane. They married quickly. Husband number 3, Henry Dawson was very wealthy, a member of the show committee and race clubs committees. Elaine had no interest in horse racing but attended all balls and functions with him. It was said he showed her off like a prize possession. Leaving the race track after a meeting and long session in the members' bar, he was run down in the car park by a hit and run driver. Neither the car nor the driver was ever found.

'Collins was sure the next one she married would be the driver of the car that killed husband number three, Henry Dawson. In his spare time, Collins had discovered the dead real estate agent, Busby, husband, number 2, was a passenger on the cruise ship from which her first husband, Davies, had gone missing. Collins had a theory the real estate agent had killed her first husband on the promise of marriage and a share of the life policy. The woman had then killed the real estate agent to close the circle. He was sure the Coroner must have got it wrong.

'After the grazier's death, Elaine Williams married a high rise rigger who had subsequently fallen from the tenth floor of the unit she now owned. Collins declared him the murderer of Dawson, but we found no contact between him and Elaine before the hit and run killing. Close questioning of his friends revealed they thought he had screwed his way into money, as he had only modest means. Collins believed Elaine had closed the circle by murdering the real estate salesman and rigger.

'The rigger had fallen to his death showing a crowd at a party at the unit what he did at work, by walking around the edge of the unit balcony. Heavy rain next day wiped out anything that made him slip and plunge to his death. Husband number 4. Collins was confident he was on the money this time. An inquest found accidental death. Coincidence again? Hardly. But why? Collins was pestering me.

'A year later, she married a national developer who had divorced his wife and fallen out with his adult children in order to marry her. He was much older than her, but they are still married. She was a real looker and femme fatale who knew how to use her charm and looks. Husband number five. That's it. We found nothing but coincidences, but Collins became obsessed with it and would not let it go. He became a pest. But recollecting it, I have to wonder if he was right?'

After a few moments, Findlay mused, 'Yeah, a lot of coincidences, but the fifth marriage is stable. Collins says it's because her present husband has all his assets in trusts and his family are the trustees. His wealth is out of her reach. Or alternately, she is rich enough not to need more money. Her husband gives her entrance to high society and she is a social butterfly. That's all I have, Vergil.'

'What was your assessment of Collins?' asked Rankin

'A tenacious investigator. He never took a sick day. His diligence and dedication cost him his wife and family. He now has grown children who don't come near him, as he didn't give them the time they deserved when they were young. Beware, Rankin.'

They shook hands and parted like old friends. Rankin went back to his office.

Findlay's recollections were interesting – so many coincidences, but no proof sufficient to persuade a coroner. He rang Collins and told him he had seen Findlay and would pull and read all reports on the cases and get back to him if he had any queries. Collins offered to come to the office and help him, but Rankin declined the offer.

***

Later in the day, the files covering the four deaths hit Rankin's empty desk. Elaine Jane Williams, 21, had married Arthur Brian Davies a widower with no children, who lived with his spinster sister at Woollahra in Sydney.

The CIB investigation of the cruise ship disclosed that Arthur Davies rarely left his first class cabin during the two week cruise. The cabin steward told police that he had made the missing passenger's bed the day before the ship docked. Police had made a thorough search of the ship. The Coroner's report was clear.

Ivan Collins always believed Elaine Williams was involved in Arthur Davies disappearance, the life insurance policy proceeds made it all so obvious. In his spare time, Collins had checked the backgrounds of both husbands looking for a connection of some kind. Husband number 2 was listed as a passenger on the cruise ship. He had also been the selling agent who located the home unit in which the Williams had lived. They married. He died three months later from a heart attack.

Notwithstanding the Coroner's findings, Collins believed husband number 2 had been involved in the disappearance of husband number 1. Therefore, it followed that Elaine Williams was most probably involved in the death of husband number 2.

Nevertheless, the Coroner found that Elaine Williams did not benefit financially or otherwise from the death of Busby. But Collins believed that with the death of husband number 2, Elaine had now closed the circle and only she knew the truth.

Facts could not be found to support Collins' theory that Busby had gained access to Arthur Davies' cabin, overpowered Davies, a much older man, then heaved him over the outside railing of the ship into the ocean – all achieved outside the scope of the security cameras. Collins believed that Busby was smart enough to run the shower, leave wet towels on the bathroom floor, and quickly rumple the bed.

After marrying husband number 3, Henry Dawson, again a much older, successful man, Elaine Williams began life in a heritage home on Hamilton Hill with views of the Brisbane River from her veranda.

47

Six months later, Henry Dawson was dead, victim of a hit and run driver as he was walking to his car parked at the race club member's car park. Dawson had attended a member's dinner. Elaine Williams was attending a fund raising dinner at the time of his death. Findlay and Collins suspicions were aroused, but could find no evidence to support Elaine's role in his death.

The CIB were called in to investigate Dawson's death. No witnesses came forward. Neither the car nor its driver was found. Another referral to the Coroner.

File notes showed that Collins believed that husband number 4, Glen Albert Barrett, a high rise rigger, had to be somehow involved in Dawson's death. What was the appeal of such a rough neck? Three short marriages, each resulting in mysterious, and in some cases violent death – what had been the point of the marriages?

Some three months after her marriage to Glen Barrett, Elaine was widowed for the fourth time. Barrett's mates said he was an accident waiting to happen. During a party, Barrett slipped and fell to his death while lairising on the tenth floor outside ledge of the unit in which he and Elaine lived. The unit had been purchased by Elaine after she sold the Hamilton house following Henry Dawson's death.

Sometime after the marriage between Elaine Williams and Glen Barrett, Police interviewed Barrett's mates in relation to Barrett's movements on the day of Henry Dawson's death. An alibi was quickly produced. Six of them were at the races the day of the hit and run killing of Henry Dawson.

They drank at the public bar at the track until six pm and then got taxies to the Breakfast Creek Hotel. They continued on there until ten o'clock that evening then got taxies to Sybil's night club in the city, staying there until it closed at 3am. All stated Barrett was with them at all times, but all were drunk.

Was it a case of the parts amounting to less than the whole? The Coroner could only rule on the evidence presented by Police Prosecutors in respect of each death. In theory, Collins was right to draw the inference that Elaine Williams was involved to some degree in each murder, but extensive investigations had not produced sufficient evidence to support criminal charges.

CIB's thoughts on the investigation would be useful. As a last resort, Rankin rang the retired Chief of CIB, Brady, saying he was working on a case on which Brady may be able to assist – the hit and run killing of Henry Dawson at the race course car park. Brady offered to come to police headquarters to discuss the file. Rankin preferred to see Brady at his retirement unit at Redcliffe.

Whilst waiting for Rankin to arrive, Brady had time to marshal his thoughts.

Rankin arrived and Brady and his wife welcomed him at the front door; a pot of tea and a plate of biscuits were quickly produced. Brady's account pretty much matched Findlay's recollections.

Echoing Collins' suspicions, Brady surmised that Busby murdered Davies at sea; Elaine Williams then married Busby as agreed and when he died, the circle was closed; she was free of any problem that he might cause her.

49

'She then married Dawson, a man of real wealth, who was subsequently run down and killed by a hit and run driver. Homicide and my department carried out a massive search for the vehicle and driver. We checked every panel beater and wrecking yard. Glass found at the scene was believed to have come from a Ford Fairlane. Our intense investigation uncovered a lot of fraud in the used car industry and wrecking yards, but not the car we were looking for. Elaine Williams was now a wealthy woman. She then married a construction worker Barrett who fell to his death from the tenth floor of the unit they lived in during a party she had arranged.

'Collins believed Barrett had murdered Dawson but he had an alibi for the time of the killing and when he fell to his death Collins believed she had again closed the circle. She became the mistress of a very wealthy developer and builder who then divorced his wife and married Elaine. Collins never gave up.

'Collins' inquiries found that the developer, Hans Christenson had his wealth held in trusts to which she had no entitlement; hence no benefit in having him killed. Elaine was now in the big time – rich by marriage, has entry into high society, which she floats through as a social butterfly. She is now mixing with the rich and famous, and had strong political connections. She is a big donor at election times.'

Rankin heard Brady out and then said, 'I was contacted by Collins. What is your assessment of him?'

Brady replied, 'A very good detective who became obsessed with Elaine Williams.'

After a while, Rankin nodded and said, 'She has an interesting past. Do you think Collins could have been right?'

Brady replied, 'There was no proof, only suspicions, but Dawson's death led to a clean-up in the used car and panel beating businesses. We uncovered fraud against insurance companies, stolen cars repainted and sold, cars hired out to people committing robberies. Once nailed, most gave up their accomplices for favourable reports on how helpful and cooperative they had been. We had a real clean up and nailed six people involved in robberies and the firm who supplied the cars for them. The vehicle supplier owned a wrecking yard and a car crusher. Vehicles used in robberies were older cars dumped at his yard, stripped, and put through the crusher – reduced to iron, usually bound for Japan. No DNA or fingerprints are available after that. A panel beater's shop owner would contact the car supplier and arrange the car for a robbery. They would organise where to leave it for pick-up and where they would leave it when they had finished. Elaine Williams lost our interest, but not Collins.'

Sitting back in his office chair later, a light was flickering in Rankin's brain. Something Brady had said was important, but his thoughts were interrupted by the phone ringing. It was Deputy Commissioner Larson. Rankin had another case to go to. He had to put his investigation into Elaine Williams on hold.

CHAPTER 3

SATANIC MURDERS

Rankin was in his office when a phone call was put through to him. The caller was a detective sergeant from Toorbul, a city suburb. The caller, Detective Burgess said there had been a murder there and he believed it required Rankin's squad to handle it. Rankin and Henderson drove to the address given by Burgess.

Burgess met them at the garage door to a low block brick house. There was a police tape across the open garage door. Plastic-suited, Rankin and Black entered the taped off area after forensics had finished their examination of the body. All photographs had been taken and the room dusted for finger prints.

Mullins, the State Forensics Officer was standing amidst an extraordinary scene. 'Bad one, Rankin,' Mullins observed, still looking around the room. 'Looks like a satanic murder. The victim was strangled, and desecrated after death; candles were lit beside the body. Murdered Friday night, I believe, but that's only a guess until I get her to the morgue. No evidence of sexual assault. Desecration of her body was by a sharp weapon, probably a cut throat razor, wiped clean on her blouse. Never seen one like this before.'

Rankin examined the woman on the floor. She was dressed in shorts, a short sleeved top, and tennis shoes. Her hands were folded on her stomach. Her tongue was bitten.

A small amount of blood from it was on her heavily bruised neck. There was a thin line of blood from her forehead to her navel and shoulder to shoulder, a small cross was cut on the forehead, long at the navel. An inverted small crucifix was in her mouth. The cuts formed a rough cross. Candles had been lit on each side of the body and were now just a pool of wax at their plastic bases. A small hand bag and a set of keys were beside the body.

'Don't like it, Chief,' said Henderson. .

'Not much blood on the body,' said Rankin.

Mullins replied, 'Heart had stopped beating after she was strangled, possibly by a thin leather strip or belt. It was no longer pumping blood when the cuts were made. The killer must have had a light to do the desecrations, as the room would have been dark. Probably by candle light from the two candles each side of her dead body.'

The body was taken to the city morgue. Rankin remained in the room, studying it carefully. The handbag had a wallet that contained money, club membership cards, and her driver's license. A small towel and a small key were nearby. The keys were for a car, house doors, and possibly a locker door. He thought it most likely, that the victim had driven into her garage after opening the tilt-a-door, left her vehicle, which gave off two minutes of light, closed the garage door and gone into her lounge through the door from the garage. Rankin checked the main entrance door to the house. The killer could have been in the house waiting for her. The front door was a standard lock. Easily opened by even a bankcard.

53

Rankin flicked the switch of the light near the doorway into the lounge. It didn't come on. Investigation showed the bulb was missing. She had entered the lounge and gone to the kitchen to turn its light on, but had been strangled before she reached it. There was evidence of a struggle. A quick search of lounge and kitchen of the house revealed nothing of interest. He saw a tape player, classic music, books, TV, and a neat clean kitchen.

The car had been dusted on the outside and Rankin opened the door with its key. In the glove box was the vehicle's registration papers, vehicle manual and a tennis racket on the back seat.

Uniformed police were calling house to house in the street where she lived. CIB and members of the local homicide had interviewed her fellow teachers, known friends, and all members of the clubs she belonged to.

Three days after the discovery of the murder, Rankin set up an incident board in a room on his floor at State Police Headquarters, and called a meeting of his team – senior officers of CIB and uniformed police. Deputy Police Commissioner Larson was in attendance. Reports had come in with statements of her fellow teachers, friends, people she played tennis with two nights a week, and neighbours. All reports had been carefully read by Rankin and his team. His whiteboard contained all that they knew.

Name of victim: Donna May Roxon. Age forty nine. Where killed: 14 Lucas Street, Toorbul.

When murdered: Forensic believe last Friday night.

How murdered: Strangled, body desecrated after death.

Who murdered her and why: Unknown.

Rankin said, 'Known facts about her to date – high school teacher, age forty-nine, divorced, three adult children living out of the state. She had an active social life – tennis player, member of little theatre, and had many close friends. Not a church goer. A Saturday morning shopper at the local supermarket.

The body was discovered by her school principal, who was concerned when she did not turn up for work Monday or ring to say she would not be in. The principal stated she was very reliable. At the lunch break, he went to her home. When his pressing the front door buzzer and knocking on the door got no answer, he forced opened her garage door. Her car was there. He was very concerned, so he opened the unlocked door to the lounge, found her body, and contacted police. A senior sergeant and constable had gone to her house, taped off the murder scene, and called the local homicide team. One of them contacted us. All her neighbours have been interviewed by a house-to-house police investigation by a large number of uniformed police and CIB. They had interviewed all teachers, friends, and tennis club members. All reports were in.'

For effect, Rankin attached a blown-up photo of the victim to the whiteboard and asked for opinions. Leading off, Deputy Commissioner Larson said, 'A ritual sacrifice. Is a real weirdo on the loose out there?'

Rankin nodded his face grim. 'I rang the uni and found a professor who was expert on the occult. I was informed there are countries in West Africa that have Christian and Muslims religions living side by side.

'Between them, they have sects and devil worshippers. This fits their pattern. Black candles mean a human offering with no sexual activity, red candles would mean many rapes before death by stabbing or throat cut, but there is always a young girl sacrificed in both cases. The mature woman is an oddity. The desecration of the body states a sacrifice to evil, defying the Christian god. The cross in her mouth inverted, the Christian sign of the cross reversed if you work it from the navel and the cut across the end of the blood line'.

Connors said, 'The Christian sign of the cross that starts at the forehead is reversed and finishes at the forehead.'

Rankin continued, 'The inverted crucifix denotes a Christian God and defies him. This could be the first sacrifice, possibly with more to come until the black God is satisfied. Mullins has stated the black candles had black boot polish on them. They were white before they were stained. If the murderer was a black African, he would have stood out, but I believe he is white and obscure. He fits in where he goes. I think he planned this murder carefully. Leaves no finger prints or shoe marks. Gloved hands and plastic covered shoes. '

There was silence in the room. It was broken by Kennedy, 'Christ, what have we got here?'

Larson said, 'A bad one – a fanatic lunatic at large. And I believe there will be more of these unless we apprehend this deranged odd ball.'

Rankin said, 'From all reports the victim led an active life and had no enemies. Her divorced husband lives in

England. She has two men in her life, both casual with no commitment, both cleared.'

'Did they know about one another?' Black asked.

Rankin nodded. 'Yes, but as stated, they both had a causal relationship with her. 'I believe we have a lot of work here eliminating every one she had contact with.'

Rankin said to Turner, 'We need all the help CIB can give us. My men will work with you.'

Everyone left the briefing room. Returning to his office, Rankin telephoned Findlay, his old boss, putting him the picture. Findlay had not encountered anything like this murder in his time in homicide.

The press were now aware it was no run-of-the-mill murder and had got information of the ritual element involved. Papers and TV were having a field day. Ink heads and talking air heads on TV were advancing way-out theories and causing a reign of terror in the suburb where the murder had happened and across the city. But the story ran out of steam in a week. However, the pressure remained on Rankin and his team.

Rankin got the phone call he had been dreading sixteen days later – another ritual murder at Redbank, west of the city and miles from the first one. Rankin and Kennedy arrived at the murder scene. The small house had the porch light still on. The forensic team had finished and the detectives entered the house. Inside, the victim had been killed and the body mutilated the same as Roxon – strangled, body mutilations, inverted crucifix in mouth, candles black waxed. No footprints or fingerprints. A purse and door keys were found in the room. The murdered woman had been identified as

Shirley Ann Gettens, age thirty-nine, single. She worked at a fast food outlet at the local shopping centre.

Uniforms, CIB, and homicide were back on the job interviewing neighbours, friends, and her fellow employees. She lived in a small house in a quiet street. . Friday night had been spent at the local tavern with her sister and friends. She had been dropped off at her residence around midnight when the tavern closed. Her sister stated the porch light was on when they left her. She also barrel bolted the back door when she was out of the house and the front door after she entered the house at night.

Police had established that her habits seemed entrenched. She worked Monday to Friday, and worked in her garden after work. Saturday she shopped with her sister. Later, both visited her mother in an old person's home and spent the afternoon there. Sunday she was a volunteer at the local football club. Apart from bar work, she took the players' jumpers home and put them through her washer. They were neatly stacked on a table. When a club member had called to take her to the match, he knocked. The front door light was on. After no answer, he went to the back door of the building, which was unlocked, opened it, and went into the house calling her name. He discovered her body and rang the police, who immediately swung into action.

The club was her only sporting connection. She didn't belong to a church.

At the crime scene, Rankin said to Kennedy, 'Same as the other one, killed and body mutilated after death by a sharp instrument that was cleaned on her clothing. Rankin believed she had opened the front door, turned on the light switch inside the door, from which the bulb had been removed, and in the semi-darkness from the light on the porch, reached for the kitchen light switch, but was killed before she got there. The killer worked in the dark or by candle light.

The fact that the porch light was still on was odd. The killer could have been noticed opening the front door, but the unlocked back door told the detectives how he avoided it. Turn off the power at the outside fuse box and enter the front door in the dark. Unbolt the back door, turn on the power, and wait for his victim. Everything would appear normal when the victim got home. A search of her unit produced nothing out the ordinary. Just a TV, record player, jazz and blues records, women's magazines, and nothing odd in the medicine cabinet.

Rankin dreaded the near future and the media storm that was growing strength. Women living alone were frightened and the press played on this. The City was living in fear fanned by the press, the ritual killings added to everyone's anxiety. Two days later, the massive police operation had got nowhere, but had eliminated many suspects.

The newspapers and TV were now giving the murders full coverage. Wild assertions of evil sects living in the city, hysterical headlines proclaiming a serial killer was loose in the city and asking who would be next if the police did not apprehend this monster, had many women terrified. Wirth, the Police Commissioner, was under press attack as was Rankin. A reign of terror spread through the city. Almost every talking head on TV and newspaper ink head was now an expert on Satanism. Predictions of copy-cat killings went into overdrive.

Rankin called another meeting of his team and department heads, but no one had anything of value to add. Larson said, 'The killer's a lunatic. No woman's safe.'

Rankin stared off into space nodding thoughtfully and said, 'He plans his actions. He knows his victims habits, he studies them, must stalk them, but we have no evidence of this. He must observe them, probably over a period of time. These are not random murders. What we know of him is that he murders on Friday night. The uni professor believes this is important. God Friday is firmly a Christian belief. He ridicules it, by offering his sacrifice on a Friday.'

After everyone had left, Rankin sat pondering the two murders. He had to offer some theories to his Commissioner. In the past, his hunches had served him well.

Massive police investigations in both cases had found nothing of real value.

The victims were two women of totally different backgrounds with nothing in common, except they were female and lived alone. Something flickered in his brain – Saturday morning shopping. They both did it, but then so did Rhonda, his wife, and thousands of other women. The murderer could have stalked them from there. But why? What had these two women done? You can't learn much about their habits unless you have time to spare, and continual stalking ran the risk of being noticed. This could have been noted and passed on to them during the two Investigations. The reports would have to be rechecked.

Two weeks later, Clayton's uniformed men had gone back to other duties and Turner had reduced his CIB officers as there were other crimes needing their attention.

The Roxon investigation had hit a dead end and the Gettens' murder was over two weeks old with no real suspects in the frame.

Rankin visited both shopping centres used by the murdered women. Both had underground and above ground car parking areas. They were busy even though it was midweek. A lot of small businesses, as well as the major retailers, Woolworth and Coles, made up the centres. He passed the takeaway where Shirley had worked. Most shoppers were busy with shopping lists. A few went to a coffee shop with friends. There were several stands in the large aisle selling organic food, health medicine, hats, and paintings. All rubbish, in Rankin's view, however, popular with many shoppers.

The key to the two murders could lie in the shopping centres. A thought crossed Rankin's mind. His team were instructed to find out from centre management all casual tenants who hired temporary space in the last year, to find them, and question them about their whereabouts on the night of the murders. After a week, they were cross-sectioning all information. One tenant was at all supermarkets late last year and early this year. He was a hat seller, William Wright, who lived in Brisbane. He had no criminal record. He had come to Australia from Cape Town in Africa twelve year ago and was now a naturalised Australian. He had been a policeman in Cape

Town. He had joined the state police and worked in CIB in a number of towns. He had been inveigled out of the force after a bad car accident and months in hospital. He had suffered post-accident trauma and spent time in a special hospital. He was on a pension and sold hats in the supermarket from an open stand. He only worked the summer months – Christmas and early new year, at the beach centres, and then closed shop when the summer ended. Rankin believed the two murders were well-planned and the murderer was a patient person. Thankfully, the press were moving on to other events.

Rankin and his team were now on their own. They were tired and frustrated, but now had something to work on – William Wright, the hat seller.

He lived at Oxley in a small unit and drove a utility. He had a shed rented to hold his merchandise. Rankin's team had learnt this from neighbours, who all spoke well of him. He was a loner, but always polite.

He came home after each working day and did not go out much then or in his off-season. He was a member of the local RSL and spent odd days and some nights there. Rankin thought Wright, as ex-police, would have knowledge of police procedure and forensics, and known how to cover his tracks. He and Kennedy visited Wright at his unit and questioned him about his whereabouts at the time of the murders. Wright was nonplussed and vague, and then refused to answer any questions. They asked to search his unit and storage shed but were rebuffed. Kennedy stayed outside the building as Rankin got a warrant.

Rankin returned and Kennedy stated Wright had a visitor who had arrived thirty minutes earlier. They entered the unit. The door was open.

A hard-faced man was with Wright. He said, 'My name is Ford. I am Mr Wright's solicitor. Why are you harassing him?'

Kennedy said, 'He refuses to answer our questions.'

Ford said, 'He is entitled to remain silent until legally represented.'

Rankin said, 'As he is, now will he answer our questions?'

'No,' said Ford, 'Not until he knows what this is about.'

Kennedy said, 'It's about the satanic murders, as your client is aware.'

Ford said, 'I know you are desperate to solve them, but my client won't be fitted up to ease the pressure on your department.'

Kennedy said, 'We don't fit people up.'

Ford said, 'I was a copper before becoming a solicitor and know the procedure.'

Rankin let it go through to the keeper and produced the two search warrants. Ford said, 'My client and I will be with you the whole time. As I said, my client won't be fitted up with planted evidence.'

A search of the unit revealed nothing of interest. A search of his shed revealed a lot of hats and sun cream, all in plastic dust covers, and a large roll of plastic. Rankin found nothing there, but a search of his vehicle revealed a pocket knife with sharp blades. Rankin bagged it and asked Wright, 'What is this used for?'

Ford said, 'Don't answer that.'

Rankin found a sharpening stone in a kitchen draw and gave Wright a receipt for the knife and sharpener. Both detectives left. Rankin sent both articles to the forensic department. He was advised next day there was nothing on the knife blades, except rope fibres and what appeared to be finger and toenail residue. The sharpener was the same. Both articles were returned to Wright. Back at their officer, Rankin set up an incident board on Wright.

An ex-policeman: mental issues in the past. Came from South Africa.

He refused to give his whereabouts at the times of the murders and they had no idea where he was at the time. A twenty-four watch was put on him. Then a 3am phone call to Rankin, at home in bed, was the call he had been dreading – another satanic murder. But this one was out of the Brisbane area. The town of Kingaroy was two hour's drive from the capital and it had no commercial air service. Wright had been under surveillance and had not left his unit that night. He was out of the frame. *A time-wasting investigation*, Rankin thought.

The Kingaroy senior detective, Browning, had given Rankin the bare details of the murder during the telephone call. Colleen Joan Morgan was around fifty years of age. Her husband worked at the coal mine in the area and she worked at a hot bread shop in the main shopping centre. She lived across the street from its main entrance. She was discovered by her husband when he finished work at midnight. Browning went on to describe the murder scene to Rankin. Her murder was the same as the other two, strangled, inverted crucifix in mouth and her body mutilated.

'She had gone to work Friday at two pm. Friday night, the centre stayed open until nine pm. Her husband had left at three-thirty to go to work, half an hour's drive away. He had arrived home at 12.30am to find her mutilated body. It was half an hour before he rang the police. He was now under sedation at one of his friend's home. The couple had no children and had been married for thirty years. A check on her husband showed he had not left work before midnight.

Rankin thanked Browning for his detailed report. His wife made a pot of tea and some toast while he rang his team. At 6am, they left by car for Kingaroy. Connors, Black, and Doyle went with him. Kennedy was left in charge at Brisbane. A little over two hours later, they were at the Kingaroy police station.

Most police in the town and nearby towns were questioning neighbours, people she worked with, and known friends. Chief Detective Browning and Senior Sergeant Evans had waited until 8am before commencing house-to-house questioning. Two constables at the station were taking phone calls. The local radio station informed the listening public of the murder and put out a police call for any assistance.

Rankin went to the murder scene, which had been taped off. Senior Sergeant Evans had answered the call from the victim's husband and secured the murder scene. Some neighbours and people from passing vehicles had been attracted to the house by police activity.

He had left the constable there to ensure no one entered the yard or house. The local forensic officer, Bruce, had been at the site.

It had been dusted for prints, and photos were taken, but Rankin wanted Mullins at the scene. A call to Commissioner Wirth at 7am from a roadside public phone, as his car mobile was out of range, got what he wanted.

Together with Connors, he inspected the murder scene, but they did not enter the taped off area. The street where the victim had lived consisted of low-blocked wooden houses. Police were doing house-to-house inquiries in the street and beyond, supervised by the senior sergeant. People were gathering outside the victim's residence. It would not be long before the media arrived.

Black and Doyle were at the supermarket getting details of casual stall operators.

Senior Detective Browning was with Rankin when Mullins arrived with the local forensic officer and two assistants. Rankin, Browning, and Connors waited outside the taped off area as Mullins and his team went to work. When he had finished, he came over to Rankin, removed the plastic suit, and said, 'Number three, same MO as the other two. Bit her tongue, as did the first victim. Blood on her neck. You did not need me. Bruce did a good job.'

Rankin replied, 'It could have been a copycat murder as the press had many detail of the others.'

Mullins said, 'He has to be stopped. He is getting desperate. Murdering a woman while her husband is at work means local knowledge – more so than in a big city.'

Rankin was well aware of this, but thanked Mullins. Suited up, the homicide team entered the taped off area.

The woman lay on her back between the enclosed front porch door and the lounge room. The light bulb in the porch light had been removed. She would have turned on the porch light switch. When the light did not come on, she went for the lounge switch. She did not reach it. The murderer was waiting for her. Her house keys and two loaves of bread were in the lounge.

Police interviewed all neighbours, her friends, and shop customers. All temporary stall holders were interviewed. At midday, Rankin called a meeting of all senior police. He had set up an incident board with the victim's name, known details, and usual questions on it. He had a line through neighbours, fellow workers who were all young girls, and her close friends. The town had only one large supermarket to service a town population of around ten thousand.

Anyone odd would have been noticed here, unlike the big city shopping centres. The victim led a quiet life, went to country and western concerts, alone or with her husband or close friends. She and her husband belonged to the local Baptist church. The house search revealed a tape recorder, lots of country and western tapes, TV, women's magazines, old novels and a revolver in a locked safe. The key was under a beer coaster. Browning told them her husband belonged to the local pistol club. He took the gun and said it would be locked in the police safe until the owner had recovered from shock.

Back at the police station, Rankin arranged accommodation twelve miles out of Kingaroy as the town was booked out with the annual race meeting there that day. He outlined the MO of the murderer to Evans and Browning.

The murders were always a Friday night. Victims were strangled then the body was desecrated with a pagan symbol, an inverted Christian crucifix was placed in the mouth, black nugget coated candles burnt on each side of the body. The entrance light bulb was always removed. He told them that this murder investigation was their best chance of apprehending the murderer. A stranger would have stood out in this established town. The police knew most locals, but had no useful information. Browning said the area had its share of weirdos, but they were not up to this. Everyone was at a loss to explain the brutal murder. They agreed it was not a crime of passion.

Rankin thought about the other murders, and the links between them. All were committed Friday night, same MO. He knew the murders were not random. They were well-planned and executed. The murderer had to know their habits, and maybe them, but there was no common denominator except they were females, two worked at supermarkets, two shopped there Saturdays.

This investigation was going nowhere, as had the others. He stated that the murderer had to be someone from the shopping centre or someone who had ties to it. Questioning of stall holders had yielded nothing of importance. Police were being reduced as there was a race meeting today, but a number went back to questioning people with his team and Browning.

Rankin sent Doyle and Black back to Brisbane on Monday. He and Connors remained in the town.

By Wednesday, despite questioning hundreds of people, the investigation had gone nowhere.

Two young constables had been left at the Kingaroy police station to man the phone. The press – TV, and local radio – had reported the murder and a police call for information had resulted in many calls to the police station, which was now vacant except for Rankin, Connors and the constables.

Rankin went back to the shopping centre. It was not busy, but would be tomorrow, pension day.

Rankin and Connors went to the shopping centre the next day. It was busy.

He noticed a road-side business outside the main car park.

He asked the senior sergeant about it, as he had not noticed it at any of the city shopping centres. The Sergeant said, 'The supermarket attracts people in large numbers. Small time business people could use the supermarket's ability to attract customers for their own benefit. Organic vegetable growers, ornamental tree sellers, key cutters, coffee vans, and cheap trinket and clothing sellers all set up at the main entrances to shopping centre parking area.

'They pay no rent but benefit from the crowds the supermarkets draw. Many come and go, but some come on a regular basis, fortnightly, or monthly. The local police are used to them and don't notice them. We have all their vehicle number plates. The shopping centre clients want them moved, but if we do that all charities that use streets and footpaths will have to move.'

With this new information, Rankin contacted Browning and Connors, asking them to come to the station.

When they arrived, he stated he wanted all people who operated businesses outside the supermarket to be checked and questioned about their whereabouts the night of the murder. When he had finished, a sceptical Browning commented, 'Most are locals, but there are a few regular outsiders.'

Rankin said, 'I want a list of them all today. The murderer is from out of this town.'

'All theory,' replied Browning, 'but we will get on with it.'

As Rankin and Connors left the police station, they steadfastly ignored the press at the fence yelling questions at them. Evans arrived at the station as they were entering their car and said, 'To most people at the races, the murder was a topic of conversation, but punters had little interest after the races started. To most of them, what's going to win the next race is their main concern. But a number of worried women approached me. This area will now be a centre of fear.'

Rankin nodded grimly. 'With good reason.' He and Connors drove back to Brisbane.

Rankin gave his report to Wirth and spent the weekend at home with his family. A day trip to the north coast won brownie points from his wife and sons.

Monday morning, he was at his office early. The newspapers and TV had sensational lead stories. "Where would the monster strike next", they asked. The Burnet area was in a state of fear.

He had set up an incident board, condensing the known facts of the three murders. Browning rang from Kingaroy and gave him five names of people who visited the town spasmodically and had been coming there for years.

A district vegetable farm owned by Asians sold their produce twice a year outside the supermarket car park, a van was there occasionally selling cheap clothing, a key cutter and knife sharpener set up business outside the car park once in a while, a seafood seller was very popular and much cheaper that local outlets. He came from the central coast.

A van with gaudy jewellery was very popular among the young people when it came there. He gave Rankin their number plate information, which they had recorded in case of trouble. All were from outside of Brisbane except the key cutter and knife sharpener. All would have to be investigated by the police in their towns. The key cutter and knife sharpener they would handle. Browning told him that people in the same business in the shopping centre resented them.

They were considered free-loaders. The shop keepers paid high rents for their shops and the free-loaders paid none. A lot of them slept in their vans using service station showers. Rankin added this information on to the incident board. He sent Kennedy to profile Large, the key cutter and knife sharpener. Kennedy established his work pattern, where he lived, and the number of a second car at his unit, which was in a block of four that he owned. He rented out the other three.

71

He had no police record and had come to Australia fifteen year ago from South Africa, where he had been a police man then a member of a special army squad. He set up a security firm here, which he sold five year ago, and bought his present business.

He was a member of the local tenpin bowling club and darts club, which met Tuesday and Thursday nights. Despite his clean record, Rankin wanted a watch on him Friday night, as he had arranged with outside police for the other casual supermarket car park business operators. Rankin was taking no chances. The officers watching the key and knife man reported that Large had fixed habits. Darts at the local Tuesday night, ten pin bowling Thursday night, and horse races Saturday, after a morning cutting keys and sharpening knives at some large supermarket where vendors like him and his van did not stand out. Connors took two knifes to Large to be sharpened. Connors did not look like a policeman. Connors reported Large was friendly and talkative. Beside the sharpening and key cutting, Large sold candles and holders. He told Connors people bought them for romantic candlelight dinners and wedding reminders. After a month, all surveillance was called off on all suspects. All seemed to lead normal lives. There were no further satanic murders for six weeks.

Then Rankin's home phone rang at 2am Saturday morning. He was tired, but came to life quickly. There had been another ritual murder at Redcliffe, down at the bay.

He rang Connors, and, collecting him at the station, he drove to Redcliffe.

There were police cars outside a cottage on Anzac Avenue, about two hundred yards from the town esplanade. The local forensic officer, photographer, and finger print man had completed their work. Daley, the forensic officer, had waited for homicide to arrive. The front room of the house was taped off. Rankin and Connors entered the taped off area with Daley.

The familiar scene greeted them – a female person about fifty-years-of-age, dressed modestly, strangled, body violated, inverted crucifix in her mouth. Her small handbag and two keys on a small ring lay beside her. The handbag contained tissues and lunch wrap. The enclosed porch light bulb had been removed, but the light in the passageway and front bedroom had been switched on, so police could see.

A large print of Christ that hung on the left wall had been cut and was now tattered. Two large photos of men either side of it were intact. On the other wall of the porch were photos of a large post office and a group of many men.

Connors said, 'The post office was the site of the Irish Revolution in 1922. Great speeches of freedom from English tyranny by Pearce and others were given that day. The photos on each side of Jesus Christ are Daniel O'Connor, an English man who supported Irish independence and was hung for it. Collins, on the other side, was the first elected president after Southern Ireland gained its freedom in 1924. He was assassinated by his own countrymen. Just thought my knowledge of Irish history could be helpful.'

A search of the house revealed old solid fixtures and catholic newspapers. Christ crucified on the cross was in every room. Small statues of the Virgin Mary and a large bible were also found.

Ryan, the senior CIB detective based at Redcliffe, was waiting for Rankin outside the taped off area. When Rankin joined him, he gave a brief sketch of events and the background of the victim. She was a seven-day-a-week church goer. When she had not turned up for mass this morning, the priest had come to her house, which was close to the church. The front door was open and he entered the house calling her name. He found her, rang the police, and waited for them to arrive. The priest was waiting at the church to see Rankin.

The priest was Irish, in his sixties, and a rough and tumble commanding man. He gave Rankin and Connors the details of the murdered woman.

'Her name was Mary Colleen Collins. She was fifty-years-old. She had nursed a sick father for twenty years. Before that, she had done housework for her family. Her father was a severe diabetic. He lived for years because of her attention to diet, tablets and his need of insulin. He was an Irish catholic, bigoted, anti-British, anti-protestant, and went with his daughter to mass and communion every day.

'When he was ill, communion was brought to the house. His only relief was his bible, which he read regularly. He often challenged my sermons in private. Mass every morning, communion every day, and rosary each night, was their life.

'She cleaned the church, but looking after him, taking him to lay flowers on his wife, her mother's, grave near the church on Sunday was her life for twenty years. He is now buried next to his wife. She took flowers to their graves three times a week. At forty eight, she was past marriage and bearing children. I advised her to get a job to break the monotony of her life and get more people into it.'

Rankin and Connors heard him out without interruption. He continued, 'But she had no qualifications. I got her a job at the nearby supermarket, stacking shelves three nights a week. She settled in well and got on well with other staff. The night she was murdered, she worked from when the business closed at ten pm until 1am, then rode her pushbike home, half a mile away. Except for her job, nothing changed in her life.' The priest was quiet. He had said it all.

Rankin asked, 'Any men in her life?'

The priest replied, 'No, she was shy and introverted and would have told me if there was. Why would anyone do this to her? I said the last rights over her desecrated body before I notified the police. Why put the marks of Satan on a living saint?'

Rankin thanked him and they left. Out of hearing, Connors said, 'She was everything Satan opposes. The perfect offering – a living, saintly victim. That's why it was so long between murders. The murderer wanted a perfect offering.' Rankin rang the rest of his homicide team to join them.

He set up an incident board at the Redcliffe police station with the victim's name, age, and the information given by the priest on her life.

Police had done a house-to-house and questioned everyone in her street and neighbourhood. But no one was up at a quarter past one when she would have arrived home. There would have been light traffic on the road. An appeal had gone out on radio, morning TV, and it would be in Sunday's newspapers tomorrow. There was a gathering of TV cameras and reporters at the cottage gate being held back by uniformed police. She appeared to have no close friends, except her family who had visited her and her late father. Her three work mates were interviewed. All were shocked at what had happened. She had worked well with them and occasionally they all had coffee together at a seaside café.

They had all parted from her at the supermarket after work. Offers to walk her home many times were refused good-naturedly.

Rankin did not like this one. It was worse compared to the other three, which were terrible.

Lack of friends, no social life, and strict habits were the killer's advantage if she was studied for a time. Shopping centres went through Rankins mind. They appeared to enter every equation. His team joined him and local police in Redcliff. He set up an incident board at the local police station. A theory was forming in his mind. Local police confirmed Harry Large operated outside the shopping centre where Miss Collins worked. Connors stated she was her father's daughter and would not talk to a pommy. Rankin considered it a fair point.

Harry Large operated in all large shopping centres and had to be in the frame, regardless of the fact that police investigations and surveillance had found nothing suspicious. Rankin and his team were back in Brisbane at midday. Next day was Sunday and a bad day for gathering information. At Monday's meeting, Rankin had set up an incident board with the information gathered so far. Large was back in the frame regardless of Connors' belief that Mary Collins would not have spoken to him.

Photos of Large at work and at social occasions were distributed to all officers. He looked different in both. Work clothes, hat and eye protection glasses in one photo, neat and well-dressed in the other that was taken at pub he patronised by a police photographer.

Immigration Department records disclosed that Large had entered Australia fifteen years ago on a South African passport; the details made him fifty years of age now. He was born in Nigeria in 1920. Nigeria was then a British protectorate. He remained in Nigeria until 1946 when independence was granted. Most British people left at that time.

Wednesday, Rankin had twenty photos of Large in social dress printed, along with a photo of his private car model from a car dealer. Large's number plates were affixed to the photos. Operation Large began that day.

The police were now going over ground already covered by previous investigations. The new photos of Large's car model and number plate could reveal new evidence. All people interviewed on the four murders earlier were now requestioned.

This time they were provided with copies of photos of Large in social dress, and his car type and number plate.

By Tuesday morning, there were hundreds of reports, all being carefully read by Rankin's team. Rankin wanted to tie Large to Mary Collins. He thought the shopping centre had to be the place. But questioning of staff had yielded nothing of value, except the fact that Large occasionally set up his van at the above ground car park.

The one thing positive, he thought, was that Mary Collins would not have had him in her presence. She was her father's daughter and detested Englishmen. Large could still have murdered Mary Collins, if knew her work habits. Rankin had to tie Large to the victim.

He and Connors were back at the shopping centre Wednesday, but failed to get any worthwhile evidence. They were leaving when a young man wheeled a trolley past them. He had retrieved it from the outside of the car park and was taking it to a trolley enclosure. Rankin approached him and identified himself.

The young man was not overly impressed by Rankin's badge and looked at the detectives. Shown a photo of Large and the victim, he identified both. Asked if he had seen them together, he said, 'A couple of times.' Rankin's heart missed a beat. 'When were they together?'

Garry, the trolley man said, 'A couple weeks ago, sometime. He sharpened a couple of knives for me and she was talking to him. I worked with her at times, nice old lady.'

Connors said, 'She would have hated an Englishman.'

Garry said, 'He was not English. He was the son of a Boer who fought and hated the British.'

On the way back to Brisbane, Rankin was deep in thought. They could now tie Large to Mary Collins, but that in itself was not a case for arrest.

Back at his office, he called his team together and they went through what they had. There was good response to the photos of Large and his car except for hazy identification.

Rankin did not want another Wright fiasco. They worked through what they had, which was all circumstantial. Rankin and Black went to his ground unit that afternoon. The van was not in its carport. Large was cutting the lawn. He stopped the mower and looked at them.

Rankin said, 'Police,' and produced his badge. Large said, 'Have you found the bastard who stole and torched my work vehicle?'

Rankin looked at Black and said, 'We are here to get more details.'

Large said, 'As I reported to the local police, I woke up last Saturday morning and the Kombi was gone. Monday morning it was found at the Gales Golf Course burnt out. Early golfers stated that a van had been parked at the end of the club parking area, and had burst into flames. My van had been torched.'

'Where is it now?' asked Black.

Large said, 'I called a car wrecker. It was only good for scrap iron. He has a vehicle presser. Forensic found nothing at the burn site. Everything was scorched. My two machines were wrecked beyond repair. I inspected the wreck with the police and got permission to remove it as the golf course wanted it shifted.'

Black said, 'Who was the wrecker who removed the van?'

'One of Simpson's drivers from Ipswich.'

Rankin turned to leave. 'We will stay on it.' He signalled Black to follow.

In his car, Rankin said, 'Thank God you were with me and caught on quickly. Large is an ex-policeman and would have been aware that we were senior detectives. A detective constable or uniformed police officers would have been assigned to investigate the theft of the vehicle. Let's talk to the police he called first.'

A detective constable and a uniformed constable were interviewed at Toowong police station. Their report was interesting. Inquires of neighbours in Large's street had established that two people had heard Large's van going down about 3 am Saturday morning. They recognised its distinct motor sound. Large often started early if he was going out of town. Simpson the wrecker whose driver had taken Large's burnt out to his yard was interviewed but of no help.

He said he had received a burnt out vehicle that had its inside cleaned out and it was ready to crush into iron for Japan, which he had done. The floor inside of the van was ashes and only the key cutting machine, blank keys, and candle stick holders were not turned to ashes.

The forensic officer who inspected the burnt out vehicle was interviewed and stated it was overkill. 'It had been reduced to a frame and chassis. Even the tyres had been burnt to the rims. If Large is the monster, he has luck on his side.

'Got rid of all evidence by torching the van with his murder accessories in it after killing Miss Collins.'

Rankin considered Large could have parked the Kombi in the parking area of the golf club at the end of its private road, slept in it, then used a timer or candle to set the van alight after he had caught a train that ran from Ipswich to Brisbane. There would have been people at the station early. Kennedy got the Toowong Railway Station surveillance records for Saturday morning.

The CCTV at the Toowong Railway Station revealed a man bearing a likeness to Large leaving the station by the steps that lead out of the downstairs platform, early that morning. A duck billed cap and sunglasses worn by the man confused things; nevertheless, there was a strong resemblance to Large.

Late in the afternoon, they were back at Large's unit. Shown a photo taken from the CCTV, which recorded the time of the images, Large denied it was he. But then he said he had taken his other vehicle to the city for service early Saturday morning. He had caught the train home, then back to the city.

They left him and returned to the railway station. The CCTV showed him clearly coming up the steps at 9am and going down them at four thirty. Large had everything covered. No ticket had been bought at the Gale's Railway Station from the conductor, who stated that many people were on the train and he did not recognise Large in the photo. He said he just glanced at weekly tickets.

The new photos of Large out of work clothes had a response. A waitress at a hotel in Kingaroy thought he had a meal there the night of Mrs Morgan's murder, but could not swear to it. A shopper stated a person like the one in the photo was talking to the victim that night, but again could not be sure. The members of the tennis club Mrs Roxon attended said many people watched their games, some from parked cars. None could identify Large's private vehicle. People at the disco Shirley Gettens went to, said a man like the one in the photo was often at the Friday night disco, but could not be sure it was he. Staff there stated that they only recognised trouble-makers.

Rankin thought they had a good circumstantial case against Large, but not enough to charge him. Large had luck on his side if he was the murderer.

Rankin and Black went to Large's unit at ten o'clock the next morning and knocked on his front door. Large opened it saying, 'Have you got the bastard who torched my van?'

Rankin said, 'Read my badge.'

He handed it to Large who frowned. 'There was no body in the van.'

Rankin passed a file to Large. 'We have a number of questions we want you to answer. We need to know your whereabouts on these dates.'

He studied them and said, 'I have to get my work diary from my office.'

He returned with a black book. What he had recorded married up with what the police investigation of the shopping centres had found. But he was never working where the murders were committed on the day they happened. It was always weeks before. He denied knowing any of the victims except Miss Collins.

Rankin said, 'We would like to search your house.'

'Got a search warrant?'

Rankin shook his head. 'No, but Inspector Black will remain here while I get one.'

Large sighed and gestured at the door. 'Put everything back in its place.'

The two detectives put on latex gloves. The lounge room had a recorder, marching band tapes, unlabelled tapes, which Large said were African native taped music. Books by Archer, Wilber Smith, Forsyth, and a big TV. The kitchen, like the lounge, was neat and tidy. The bathroom was clean. The medicine cabinet held nothing of interest, but a cut throat razor was in a shaving basin and a sharpening leather strap was attached to wall. Rankin bagged the razor and strap. They went to his bedroom and it had a walk in wardrobe and ensuite.

Hanging in the wardrobe was expensive clothes and shoes, black and brown shoes and hats. Large was a colour code dresser. Four belts hung from hooks, two black and two brown. Wide and thin.

Rankin gave Large a receipt for the razor and strop and the detectives left with Large saying. 'Lucky I shaved this morning. Get them back to me today or tomorrow I don't want to go to the races unshaved. Rankin sent the two evidence bags to Mullins who was at the morgue. He requested an immediate examination of them. Mullins told him he would get to it later. Rankin insisted it was urgent. Mullins took them to his lab.

Two hours later, Mullins rang Rankin. There was nothing of interest on the razor or strop. Rankin was disappointed.

All evidence was circumstantial, but blood would have been positive evidence. Rankin thought if Large had desecrated the bodies with his razor there could have been traces of victim's blood on the strop when he sharpened it. Black and Rankin went back Large's unit. He was a few minutes opening the door. He said he had been having an afternoon nap. Rankin retuned the razor and strop and both left.

Back at the office, Rankin and his team looked at all the cases and statements. Two had bitten their tongue and had blood on their necks. It could have reached the strangling weapon used, but that would have been destroyed by the van fire if Large was the killer. At four pm, they broke up and all had the rest of the weekend off unless something big came up.

Rhonda was preparing dinner when he got home. The boys had played football that morning at school in a competition and were keen to tell him about it as they had won. Rhonda was tight because he was not at the match. Rankin suggested they go up the coast after dinner and spend the night and tomorrow there. The boys agreed and Rhonda complied with their wishes. They went to Noosa and had a great weekend. He was back on side with his wife. While sitting with her in the unit where they stayed and looking over the moonlit sea, Rankin thought about the murders. The boys were at the surfer's club, which had a band.

Monday, he and Black were back at Large's unit. He was home and said, 'You are becoming a pair of pests.' Both ignored him and went to his walk-in wardrobe. Rankin took the two thin belts and turned them over.

The maker's name was inscribed on the inside of the belts. Made in the USA, Austin, Texas. The front of them had a silver buckle and two silver studs beside the usual fastener studs. Rankin bagged them and gave Large a receipt for them and they left. Rankin contacted Connors and told him to come to their office. Black would replace him on what he was now doing.

At the office, Rankin showed Connors the bagged belts. Connors said, 'The best quality available. Cost more than RM boots.'

'Who sells them in Brisbane?' asked Rankin.

'Only one outlet in the city centre. I shop there.'

Rankin had figured that, as Connors was a dresser and could afford buying there. They walked to Queen Street and entered the Myers centre. The shop Rankin wanted was called Leading Edge. They entered the shop. A young smartly dressed man was arranging a rack of trousers. Connors went to the main counter and a middle aged impeccably dressed bald man said, 'Hullo, Angus,' to Connors and eyed Rankin up. Rankin knew he had failed the dress test. He showed his badge to the man and said, 'Detective Sergeant Connors and I have a few questions for you.'

The man said, 'You a policeman, Angus? I thought you were among the idle rich.'

Rankin said, 'He is but prefers to work. Can we go to your office?' The man said, 'Certainly,' and led the way to a small office. Seated behind a small desk with Connors and Rankin seated in front he asked, 'What is this about. '

Rankin took the two belts from a bag he was carrying and said 'Were these bought here?'

The man turned them over and said, 'Yes, they have my stamp on them.' He pointed to LE in the middle of the belts. 'But the buckle holders have been modified.' He pointed to silver studs that were beside the brass clips.

Rankin said, 'You alter the buckle holders?'

The man shook his head. 'No, that would be the work of a manufacturing jeweller, to enhance the buckle.'

Rankin said, 'And strengthens the buckle holders?'

The man said, 'Yes, but why? They are very strong the way they are. It would have been altered to enhance the buckle.'

Rankin said, 'Thank you for your time.' Both detectives rose from their chairs. At the shop door, the man smiled said, 'Angus, your secret life is safe with me.'

Connors smiled. 'Good to see you, Anthony.' They left the building. The belts were delivered to the forensic department to be tested for blood stains.

Back at the office, Rankin knew this was the last throw of the dice, but he did not like his chances.

The next day the team were all back at work on other matters. That evening Rankin was having supper with the family when his police phone rang. He answered it and said, 'I have to go.'

Rhonda frowned. 'Can't it wait until tomorrow?' But he had already left the room. He was soon in his car and on his car phone to Black and Doyle. Mullins had told him there were faint traces of blood on the belts matching both women who had bitten their tongues. He picked up Black at his unit and Doyle at his house. They drove to Large's unit, but his Corolla was not in his carport.

They knew tonight was ten pin bowling night. Large appeared relaxed when they called him aside from his team. Rankin asked him to come to police headquarters. Large did not argue or ask why, but wanted to take his car home first. Doyle went with him and the other detectives followed him home. He drove his car into the carport and then he and Doyle entered Rankin's vehicle. They drove in silence to the police station.

In an interview room, they sat opposite Large who had refused legal representation. The tape recorder was running. Rankin gave all details of the reason for the interview, those present and added, 'Anything you want to tell about the murders of Mrs Roxon and Mrs Morgan, Mr Large?'

Large said, 'You're on the wrong track, Rankin.'

For the tape recording, Rankin said, 'I am showing Mr Large two belts and asking him if they are the belts detective Black and I took from his home earlier today.'

Large said, 'They look the same.'

Rankin said, 'They are very distinctive. Two silver studs holding the buckles firmly in place, besides the normal buckle clips. They have made in Austin, Texas, America on them. We found an agent who sold them in Brisbane. He stated the silver studs were added on and would have been done by a manufacturing jeweller. We dropped the said belts into our forensic department and blood samples, the same type as Donna Roxon and Colleen Morgan were found on these thin belts, behind the buckle, inside the flap, which was held on by both the standard and silver studs.

'It could not be removed unless they were broken. The blood stains were in the secured buckle wrap-over. Can you explain how they got there?'

Large said, 'Your forensic officer put the blood samples on them.'

Rankin said, 'Mr Large, we have a strong case against you. The blood stains really confirm...'

Large said, 'My God has deserted me, he is not happy with the sacrifices I have made to him and he has delivered me to you. No one but you would have had the belts examined. I thought the razor strop being cleared was the end of it. My God is unhappy with me. I have offended him and must pay the penalty. He guarded and protected me but has now deserted me. He should have enlightened me about the danger of the belts and they would have been destroyed in the van fire after I cut the buckles off. Where do I start?'

'With the Roxon murder,' said Rankin.

Large said, 'No, it starts long before that. My father worked for the British protectorate who governed Nigeria when I was born. My parents were killed in a light plane crash when I was three years old. All Brits had servants to do any work and I had a native nanny from birth, things carried on the same after their death. I had no relations. Other staff of my father's workplace had no young children and did not want me. I was left in the care of a black family. They were well paid out of my father's estate.

'I was to go to England at age fifteen to boarding school, but the depression badly affected my father's estate, which had a big shareholding, boarding school was out.

'Nigeria demanded and got independence after the war. I was in my mid-twenties at the time and working for the British government as a gofer. I had basic education from a woman in the British employment as a clerk, but I was more native than British. I had been reared with them and knew their customs and their deep religious beliefs that the Christian missions had not replaced. They accepted me as one of them. I stayed with them until I was fifteen. Then I was given a job in the embassy as a messenger boy and left the black family but stayed in contact with them. They were my real family. There was much trouble in the country between Christians, Muslims, and long-standing local native beliefs.

'After Nigeria became independent, the British left and I went with them. I went to South Africa and joined the police force\army force there. But I took all my, shall we say, voodoo beliefs with me. I was in a special squad that did not need much education to join.

'We handled things that other departments didn't have the stomach for. But eventually things got out of control, black power was in and some were calling for a trial for war crimes. I applied for entry to Australia and was successful. Three years later, I applied for citizenship, which was granted. The rest you would know.'

Rankin said, 'Harry, why kill them.'

Large said, 'My pagan God demands sacrifices for letting me live, and his wishes must be carried out. I believe he wanted one when I reached age fifty, but it had to be a young girl and I was not up for that. I decided on a number of sacrifices. At the Friday before my fiftieth birthday, Mrs Roxon died.

'The next two had to be as soon as possible. I had selected and studied a number of women for two years. I selected my victims and sacrificed them to my God as demanded. I wanted a special sacrifice for my last offering, and Mary Collins was perfect – a living saint. But I had realised I was under observation and had to wait. When surveillance was taken off me, I acted quickly. I had cut keys for all women so entry was easy.

'After the last sacrifice, I drove home in the Toyota and then left in my Kombi. I drove it to Gales, parked it at the golf course, slept in it, and got the seven o'clock train home. The van went up after I caught the train. The Kombi was set up to burn and only needed a slow burning candle to destroy it. I was on my way home in the train when it blew up. I destroyed all evidence linking me to the sacrifices –but the belts. It is the little things that bring you undone.'

Rankin said, 'Did you talk to Miss Collins? We heard she was very adverse to Englishmen.'

Large shrugged. 'Told her I was from the free-state and hated the British.' He paused for a moment then said, 'Enough talk, it is affecting my heart.' He took a tablet out of a case, rose, screamed, 'Nicarky is the true God and I now join him.' He bit down on the tablet and was dead in a few seconds.

'Jesus,' said Black, 'He had a cyanide pill in the case.'

It was over and Rankin felt cheated – a long hunt without a conviction. But now he could address the baying TV and press. Women could now relax.

Rankin closed the interview room with policemen guarding the door and rang forensic to remove the body and clean up the room.

Commissioner Wirth was advised of what had happened and was now at the station. He said to Rankin, 'Good result, Virgil. No expensive court trial.' But Rankin still felt cheated.

He drove home. Rhonda was still up, reading in the lounge. She looked at him and said, 'Vergil what's wrong, you look terrible.' He went to the bath room, had a long shower, changed into night clothes, and joined her on the lounge. He did not talk to her about cases he handled but tonight was different. Large's death in custody had unnerved him. He told her what happened and she said, 'Put it behind you, Vergil, life goes on, and the sadistic killings are over.'

He put his arm around and said, 'There are four things in my life that matter – job, you, and the boys. '

She asked, 'What comes first?'

He said nothing, as he did not have an answer. They went to bed in silence.

CHAPTER 4

WILLIAMS REVISITED

Rankin sat back on his chair and relaxed. Another file successfully closed. He was proud of the way his squad had worked on the case. He sighed and picked up a file sitting on his desk waiting for his attention. *Now back to the Williams' case.*

Casting his mind back to the previous investigation, he searched his memory. Something Brady had said was important, but he could not remember what it was. He flipped through the file. When he came to the part about the person who had supplied cars for robberies, he found what he was looking for. A panel beater, Winter, had arranged the robberies and a David John Wills had supplied the cars. Wills had been jailed for five years and his wife for six months for her part in it. He would be long out now. Rankin wanted to talk to him.

A quick check of the electoral roll disclosed a David John Wills on the state roll at an address in Ipswich. A phone number for that name was found in the phone book. He rang the number, identified himself, and asked for David John Wills. The woman who answered took a deep breath and stated he was at work.

Obtaining the address of his place of work, he took a drive from the Brisbane CBD to a business in a dreary suburb of Ipswich. It was a car wrecking yard just off the main western highway.

It had a panel beating shed, a spray painting booth, a garage opposite, and a large spare parts shop. Surrounded by a high dividing fence was a large crane, lifting car wrecks into a crusher.

Rankin showed his badge and asked to see David Wills. The office clerk said, 'I will let him know you are here.' While they waited, Rankin and Black surveyed the large shelves of new spare parts. Black said, 'Wrecking cars for parts has been superseded by new do-it-yourself kits.' The office door opened and a tall, slim man, aged about forty, with hard brown eyes, signalled them in. He indicated two chairs and sat behind his desk.

He was at ease with them, but said nothing and waited for them to open the conversation. Rankin and Black were silent. Eventually, Black broke the silence and said, 'We are here about matters that concern you.'

Wills said, 'Homicide detectives. Please explain why you are here.'

Rankin said, 'You were supplying cars for robberies a few years back.'

Wills shrugged. 'Water under the bridge, as the yanks say, done and dusted, time served and it's over.'

Continuing, Rankin said, 'According to the evidence at your trial, the panel beater arranged all hiring.'

Wills replied, 'As recorded.'

'Did anyone else ever hire from you, besides the panel beater?

Wills shook his head. 'No, he was the only contact. I didn't know who he hired it for.'

'But you knew it was for illegal purposes,' badgered Black. Wills remained silent.

Realising he had hit a sore spot, Rankin pressed harder. 'You ever deal with anyone apart from the panel beater?'

'No,' replied Wills.

Down to one word replies, Rankin thought. Softening the question, Rankin pressed on. 'We are not interested in you, but we can become interested in how you got the money to set up this operation.'

This time Wills laughed. Rising from his chair to go, he said, 'Go for it, Chief Inspector and make a real dill of yourself. Now, if you got nothing more to say, I have work.'

Feeling the momentum shift a little, Rankin barked, 'Sit down, Mr Wills, this is very serious and related to a possible murder that you could have been involved in.'

Trying not to look too interested, Wills stood by his desk for a moment. Then he sat down and replied in a subdued voice, 'Robberies, but never murder.'

Pursuing the advantage, Rankin said, 'We have no interest in you, but that could change if you lie to us.'

Wills said, 'My money came from the sale of a house on the Sydney north shore that an aunt left me in her will. I have lived down my past and am rich enough to be honest. I will say nothing that jeopardises what me and the wife have. You have nothing on me, you are just fishing, and I am not biting.'

Rankin said, 'All I want is a name and we are out of here and you won't see us again. But if you won't give us the name, we will be back each week, here and at your house. The neighbours will think you are back into something illegal.'

Wills looked hard at Rankin and said, 'I will talk to you only. Your man will leave the room.' Rankin nodded agreement and Black left the room. Not happy.

With the door closed, Wills said, 'I did hire a car, but don't know who to. He was outside my circle of usual contacts. I got a call from a man who said he wanted to hire a big car. I said I didn't understand his request. He gave a house box address which I found was a deserted house in a street of empty houses, bought by a developer, I thought he was going to build units on the land.

'He said five hundred would be taped under the box. Five hundred more would be given when the car was left at an agreed place, and then again when it was left there to be picked up by me. I went to the letter box and collected the five hundred. I delivered the car to the Breakfast Creek Hotel car park. My wife drove me home in her car. I picked up the car from the hotel car park after a phone call.

'The front was damaged and a light broken, but the five hundred was in the glove box as agreed. I drove home with one headlight and put the car back in my wrecking yard. I was not pulled over, thank God, but I would have stated someone had run into me while I was parked at the hotel, if I was. The news next morning was all about someone being killed in a hit and run at the race course car park.

'I thought it could have been my vehicle involved. I stripped it and put in the crusher. Police did arrive at my business looking for a Ford Fairlane, but there was none in my yard. The rest you know. I was shopped and convicted and have done my time. That's the story, which I will deny if you use it against me. I will state that you sent your assistant out of the room and wanted to pull a robbery and for me to supply the car.'

'Who would believe you?' said a scornful Rankin.

Wills said, 'Regardless of that, mud sticks. The new Police Commissioner has stated the police force here is clean and honest. The campaign I would run in the press would force him to suspend you at the very least. You breached police procedure by interviewing me alone and you were foolish not to carry a wire. Wills produced a small box and said, 'A wire detector, so I knew you were clean. Let's pretend this never happened. It will be best for both of us.' Wills rose. The interview was over.

Back in their car, Black said, 'What happened in the office?'

Knowing he was beaten, Rankin said, 'We can possibly tie Barrett, her fourth husband, to Dawson's murder, but not Elaine Williams.'

Rankin sent his carefully worded report to Wirth.

At a meeting in Wirth's office later in the day, Rankin told him the truth about what happened at Will's office.

Wirth heard him out and then said, 'A Mexican standoff. Leave it at that. We can do him the most harm, but he could embarrass us. Another useful aspect of the Elaine William's drama. Sometimes you never know where inquiries and hunches will end up.'

Rankin went back to his office. He was pleased with the overall result.

He rang Collins and brought him up to date. Collins said, 'You did a good job, Chief Inspector, and in the fullness time she might be brought to justice.'

Rankin took his jacket from the back of his chair and walked out of his office towards the car park and to home. A cup of tea with Rhonda sounded good.

CHAPTER 5

WINTON MURDERS

Rankin's private phone rang at eight on a Tuesday. It was only a month after the successful solving of the four Satanic murders. The caller identified himself as Detective Sergeant Morris from Winton in the far west of the state and said that three people had been shot and killed at Tedsley Downs an isolated cattle station, southeast of Winton. He stated that the killings had taken place possibly twelve days ago and there were oddities which the forensic officer did not seemed concerned about.

He said he was ringing from the cattle station in a room with a dead body, and wanted Rankin to instruct the forensic officer to leave everything until Rankin investigated them. Rankin knew procedure, but Morris was adamant that all was not as it seemed.

Morris was lucky Rankin was home and his private phone number was available with a request to telecom. Rankin rang the chief of detectives in Townsville, could not get him. But he spoke to the area superintendent, got a good report on Morris, and booked him and Black on an early flight to Emerald and from there to Winton. He rang Black to meet him at the airport at eight the next morning. Black was the best at handling this sort of operation where victims were long dead, rotten corpses.

The morning started with a quick cup of tea and toast. Rankin briefly kissed his wife, Rhonda, goodbye and drove to police headquarters in his unmarked police car.

Detective Sergeants Black and Rankin arrived at Winton at 1.00 pm. Morris, the young CIB detective sergeant stationed at Winton, and Burke, the forensic officer, met the plane.

After the introductions were made, the Brisbane detectives joined Burke, and were soon on their way to Tedsley Downs cattle station. Morris was driving. On the drive to the murder scene, Burke told Rankin that in his opinion, they were facing a murder-suicide at Tedsley Downs. He believed the property owner had shot his wife and her son, and then killed himself using a war-time, heavy, forty-five revolver. Morris stated there were oddities that had to be examined and started to tell Rankin them, but Rankin silenced him and stated he could point them out when asked too. Burke was at a loss why Harvey the station owner and had murdered his wife and her son. Morris was also a loss to understand it.

Morris said, 'It was known that Mrs Harvey had collected her son at Winton twelve days before the discovery of their bodies outside the house by two insurance men who notified the police. They stated they had not entered the house. The weekly mailman had driven past the property twice since their death, delivering mail to the mail box at the grid, but had not noticed anything out of the ordinary. The mail box was deep and he did not know if last week's mail had been collected. Harvey and his wife Gwen were often in town to shop or at cattle sales and seemed to be happily married.

'None of the three deceased had any police form, although Harvey, a licensed pilot, was often chatted for landing his Tiger Moth plane on the football grounds in the west. Local legend was that he was believed to have been a fighter pilot in the Battle for Britain. He had married a widow after he had bought Tedsley Downs. He had been in the area for ten years and married for six years.'

Rankin asked, 'Suicide note?'

'No,' replied Burke.

They drove over 60 miles of unkempt road and arrived at the station grid that had a faded sign beside it that said; 'Tedsley Downs'. There had been cattle on both sides of the road on the way out and many seven-foot posts with a wire between them. 'Party line telephone,' said Morris. A police constable was at the grid and waved them through. Morris stated two constables were left at the murder site when they had gone back to Winton after speaking to Rankin. They had been relieved this morning by two others.

A police van was at the homestead, half a mile from the grid. The road was known to be Harvey's take-off and landing strip for his Tiger Moth plane, which he and his wife used regularly to fly to Winton and cattle sales in the west. The bodies of a woman and teenage boy lay between an open garage and the homestead. They were swollen and putrid, ravaged by crows and wild dogs. Armies of black ants and flies swarmed over them. The areas had been taped off by the local police. The police photographer had recorded the scene. He was waiting in his vehicle.

Rankin, Black and Burke entered the taped off area. Morris stayed outside the tapes. Both bodies were crumpled on their sides. Rankin rolled them over. Bullet holes were still visible in both chests and exit holes in their backs. The police photographer recorded this. They were murdered between an open shed and the homestead steps.

A Tiger Moth aeroplane was anchored to the ground in the shed. Beside it was the Land Rover that Mrs Harvey had used to collect her son from Winton twelve days before the bodies had been discovered.

The detectives and Burke donned latex gloves and went up the steps to the veranda, which had squatter's chairs each side of a passage way they entered by an unlatched flyscreen door. The main entrance door was closed. The flyscreen door was closed but not locked, leaving an opening of half an inch. They walked down a passage past four bedroom doorways and entered a large room. A body was slumped over the kitchen table. 'Harvey,' said Morris who was dry reaching. The smell of dead meat was over-powering and Rankin steeled himself. Black and Burke seemed unaffected.

Decay had set in on Harvey's body. His head was resting on the kitchen table. A putrid mess had oozed from the bullet hole in the side of it and the large exit hole on the other side. Black ants were crawling over the body, and it was covered by flies – let in by the gap in the unclosed screen door. A putrid smell of decaying flesh hung in the air.

A large calibre revolver rested on the floor beneath Harvey. Morris was ashen faced and started to feel sick.

Rankin steeled himself. Black and Burke appeared unmoved by the sight.

A half-empty glass of wine rested on the kitchen table next to an opened bottle.

Rankin broke open the revolver. There were two empty shells. He turned the chamber and an empty shell was under the gun hammer. Two live bullets and an empty chamber remained. He turned until the empty chamber was under the hammer and bagged the weapon. Morris was sent to get the crew with the body bags to collect Harvey. They had now bagged the other two bodies. Rankin studied the scene. *Something is wrong here – very wrong,* Rankin thought. He asked Burke, 'Was the front door flyscreen completely closed when you got here yesterday?'

Burke replied, 'No, we left everything as it was.'

It made no sense to Rankin. Wine as the final drink when there was a bottle of Rum on a desk below the kitchen widow, The kitchen had a fireplace, large bench with cupboards below and above it, two snow queen kerosene fridges, and an a expensive, four-seat kitchen table. A gun rack above the sink held a racked rifle and scope and a small rack where the revolver had been kept. Harvey had his back to the kitchen, where the revolver was stored.

It all seemed cut and dried to Burke; however, he complied with Rankin's request for the front and back screen doors, the kitchen, and the vehicle in the shed to be dusted for prints. Experience told Rankin that in summer in the west it was unusual for the screen door not to be closed to keep flies out of the homestead.

The detectives and Burke left the room as the body was bagged. Rankin had opened the back door to the room. It had a closed screen behind it. They waited outside on the front veranda of the homestead for the smell to weaken. All bodies had been loaded into the forensic van. Burke said they would be taken to the Longreach morgue, as he did not have the facilities to do the autopsies. He wanted to confirm the same gun had killed all people.

The three detectives re-entered the big room. Harvey's removal and the opened back door had weakened the smell of rotting flesh, but it still lingered and the flies and ants were still on the table. The flies had settled where Harvey's head fluids had oozed. Rankin asked Morris, 'Was the pistol registered?' Morris replied, 'Probably not. They are used to put injured beasts down. A rifle is cumbersome. The old Sarge overlooks it as long as they don't bring them to town.'

Rankin stood behind where Harvey had been shot. Across the way were a big formal dining table and a lounge suite. A flyscreened window was between them, ten feet from the kitchen table, and in line with the window in the centre of the wall on his right. To the right of it was a desk. There was the same type of window between the kitchen sink and the office desk. An old phone was on the wall near the desk with a handle on its side to ring the exchange in Winton to be put through to any number required if the line was clear.

A number of framed photos hung on the lounge wall. One was a wedding photo with Harvey and his wife.

Another was a photo was of Harvey with an older man and young women. *Harvey's family,* Rankin thought. There was a photo of a young Harvey with two young women and another with the same young women and a middle-aged woman. A photo of a young Harvey in a flight suit beside a fighter plane hung with them. Rankin took them out of their frames and read the writing on the back of some of them. One with the young Harvey and young woman had the words, Colombo 1939, written on the back of it. The other photo of the two girls had, Dublin 1943, written on it. The photo of young pilot Harvey had, England 1940, written on it. Rankin had Morris bag the photos, and Black go through the office desk for any recent business dealings.

He then got a wine glass from a cupboard. He poured a glass and a half of water into the bottle, filling it. Rankin asker Morris what oddities about the murders he had found.

Morris said, 'Odd that he chose wine as his final drink. There was a bottle of rum and a small glass on his office desk, a much preferred final drink, and a comfortable chair. The unclosed fly screen door is odd. That seldom happens when people enter the house, but at times when the leave. Also, there is a pressure lamp beside the kitchen table. It should have been on it where it would be fired up before dark each night. It almost looked like he had a visitor that he felt obliged to be social with, but that would be odd as he did not encourage visitors – and there was no final note.'

Rankin and Black had noted the oddities but not the pressure lamp.

They digested what Morris said and left the room. Rankin had instructed the police photographer, who was still there, to take three photos of the property entrance with its name clearly shown and deliver them to the police station. He had locked the house and he would place a police tape across the entrance to the property. He went through Mrs Harvey's keys that were in her hand bag and found the keys he wanted.

Nothing more could be done at Tedsley Downs that day. The teams arrived back at Winton in early evening after a long, dusty drive.

Morris drove to the police station and helped Rankin and Black to get after hours phone numbers from the documents Black had got from Harvey's desk. Rankin thanked Morris for his assistance and told him to be at the police station at eight next morning with another officer. Black and Rankin walked the short distance to the Hotel they had booked into, The North Gregory. Black went to the bar for a long overdue drink. Rankin went to his room and showered, and went to the dining room for tea. Black joined him and they ate in silence.

Rankin went back to the police station and Black went for a walk around town. Back at the police station, after stating to the exchange operator that this was police business and not to be listened to, Rankin put a call through to Harvey's bank manager,. He had found that some operators were curious about some phone calls as were people on a party line. Rankin identified himself and informed the manager that police officers would be at his bank at 9 the next morning to talk about Gerald Harvey.

An appointment was then made with Harvey's local solicitor for 10 thirty am the next morning. Then, Rankin rang Commissioner Wirth at home and gave a brief report on the day's happenings. His final call was a quick call home.

Back at the hotel Rankin was soon in bed, pondering why a man who had everything would kill his wife, her son, and then himself. Rankin agreed with Morris that there were oddities that had to be explained. If Burke was right and it was murder and suicide, why had Harvey murdered his wife and her son?

He went to sleep thinking about them. He drifted off into an unsettled sleep.

Next morning after breakfast, Rankin and Black were at the National Bank at 9am. Black knocked on the closed door and it was opened by a stout man wearing a suit. 'David Bowden, I manage this bank,' he said extending his hand.

Both police officers shook hands with him. Bowden did not ask for badges. They were ushered into the manager's office. Bowden seated himself behind his desk with the detectives sitting in front of him.

Bowden said,   'No doubt you are here about what happened at Tedsley Downs station, dreadful business.'

Rankin, 'What do you know about Harvey?'

The manager replied, 'Financially well off, as was his wife.'

'Were you here when he arrived in the district?' asked Rankin.

'Yes,' said the manager, 'He was looking for an extensive property and found what he wanted in this district. Accounts were opened at this bank with a bank cheque for seventy thousand pounds that he said was proceeds from his late father's estate.'

Black said, 'Wasn't that unusual?'

Bowden replied, 'Not really, it saved having to transfer funds from another bank. He left it with me, and after it was cleared, he bought Tedsley Downs station.'

Black said, 'Who issued the bank cheque?'

Bowden replied, 'Harvey stated the executors of his father's estate issued it from their bank.'

'You knew Harvey socially?' asked Black.

'Not really – only as a client. Harvey didn't mix socially in the town.'

Rankin asked, 'You knew his wife?'

Bowden replied, 'Yes, she banked here and had investments in shares and hire purchase companies. She was moderately wealthy in her own right, but spent little, except on her daughter's children. She gave them a sum of money when they were born, as a legacy.'

'What was she like as a person?' asked Black.

Bowden smiled. 'The opposite to him. Bright and bubbly. They say opposites attract. They were the living proof of that. I saw her often but Harvey never entered my bank after the first meeting. His account was always in the black. All insurances were paid by bank order. Fortnightly payments were made into his three employees' bank accounts.

'Sloan, the solicitor administrator of the estate, advised me to continue paying all accounts except the life insurance payments.'

Rankin asked, 'Was Harvey's wife flirtatious?'

'No, friendly only. Why ask that question?'

Rankin said, 'When a man kills his wife there is often another man involved.'

Bowden's face flushed in anger. 'Not in this case.'

Rankin thanked Bowden for his time. Having obtained all they needed to know, the detectives left the bank.

The solicitor, Sloan, was in his office when Rankin and Black arrived at ten-fifteen. The secretary offered coffee, which they declined. At ten-thirty-five, when the solicitor's office door opened, he and a woman came out. The solicitor signalled Rankin to enter his office. Sloan was tall, hawk-nosed, and bald. Rankin and Black sat opposite him on the chairs provided. Sloan wasted no time on formalities. 'You want to know the names of the people who will benefit from the deaths of Gerald and Gwen Harvey.' Rankin nodded. 'I will release that information to you as both parties are deceased,'

Rankin said, 'Thank you. You pre-empted me.'

Sloan continued, 'Harvey left his estate to three people in equal shares, his wife, and his two sisters. Mrs Harvey left her estate to her two daughters and her son, now deceased. Harvey carried big insurance, paid by his wife to cover death duties, and loaded to cover his flying.'

Rankin asked, 'Did you know the Harvey's socially?'

Sloan replied, 'Gerald Harvey and I served on the hospital, fire brigade, and Western Development Board, but never socialised. He was difficult to know, while Gwen his wife was open and friendly.' Rankin said, 'Flirtatious?'

'Definitely not, an open friendly woman,' said Sloan. 'Back to business – after costs and death duties are paid there will be considerable money to go to their beneficiaries.'

Rankin asked, 'What will happen to the property now?'

Sloan said, 'I am the administrator and will decide that.'

Rankin said, 'Advise whoever you appoint that there are two fridges in the house that are full of perishable foodstuffs. These are the front door keys.' He handed them to Slone.

The well-ordered lives of the deceased were reflected in their wills. A list of names and addresses of beneficiaries was pinned to the cover of the office file. Sloan undertook to provide an updated list to Rankin as soon as his secretary could type it up, Sloan rose and said, 'Ring me anytime if I can be of assistance.'

After leaving the solicitor's office, Rankin went down the street to the newsagency, but today's southern papers were not in yet.

They went to the stock and station agent and met Gardner, the manager, whose company was the main supplier to stations according to the documents from Harvey's office desk. Gardner was in his office. When the detectives entered, Gardener did not ask for badges.

When the detectives were seated, he said, 'I can't understand what happened at Tedsley. They were such a close couple. We handle all his business, station supplies, general insurance on the property, cattle sales, and transport. Two of my firm's agents discovered the bodies. Dreadful business – hard to understand.'

Black asked Gardner if the company insurance agents had travelled to Tedsley by appointment. Gardner replied, 'No, just in the area. Harvey was on their list for a review of his policies. They called on the off chance that the Harveys would be home. Although they would have got short shift as Harvey did not encourage visitors and did his own reviewing. They are still suffering from shock at what they found.'

Rankin asked for his opinion of Harvey. Gardener said 'What I saw of him – aloof but not condescending. Always nodded to you, but never spoke. He paid his accounts and the people who worked for him thought him a good employer. Paid above-award wages, supplied food, tobacco, and a good home at an outstation on the adjoining property, which Harvey had also bought. But everything had to be done right. They maintained the big property. Water troughs, windmills, bore pumps, fences, helped at musters, and branded and ear-tagged all new cattle. Harvey hardly ever came near them, they informed me, and they never were invited to the homestead.

'Tedsley was a social centre when wool was king, big parties, veranda dances and a full time manager. The owners lived in the city and only visited their property during shearing time. When the bottom fell out of wool, their life changed. No income and debt increasing.

Properties like Tedsley were neglected and fell into ruin. Eventually cattle came into the area and things looked up, but never to what is was during the wool era. Harvey is the opposite to the wool people. No dances or big formal dinners with him. He does not entertain.'

Gardener was finished and Rankin asked him, 'Was Mrs Harvey a flirt.'

Gardener said angrily, 'What are you suggesting?'

Black said, 'Answer the question.'

Gardener said, 'She was a lady.'

Rankin had enough overall information for now and asked Gardner, 'Where are your insurance men now?'

Gardener said, 'In town somewhere.'

Rankin asked, 'Have you a photo of a quality bull that you could lend us?' This question surprised Gardner who reached into his office drawer. 'What breed?'

'Does not matter?' said Rankin.

'This is a Santa. You can keep it,' said Gardener.

Rankin took the photo. 'Thank you and this is not to be discussed.' Gardner nodded.

Rankin said, 'Mrs Harvey was in town the Friday she is believed to have been murdered?'

Gardener said, 'I picked up her son at the airport as instructed and he remained here until she collected him.'

Black asked, 'What was he like?'

Gardner said, 'You shouldn't speak evil about the dead, but he needed a good slapping. An ignorant, condescending upstart.'

'How would the son have got on with Harvey?'

'He would have been sent to the employees who would have educated him.'

Rankin thanked him for his help and they left the office. They had a long lunch and then went to the police station. The photos he had ordered of the property gate had been delivered to the police station. Rankin set up an incident board and listed Burke's findings and the oddities and information gathered.

There was no clear pattern. They were at a standstill until tomorrow. The senior sergeant said Burke had rung and confirmed the same gun had killed all people.

Rankin noted that on his incident board. Morris was at the station and Rankin told him, 'Tomorrow, I want the insurance men and mailman fingerprinted.

Morris said, 'They will not like it.'

'They won't know they have been fingerprinted.' He produced the three photos of the station entrance in a plastic bag saying, 'Give each man a photo, and ask him to verify that is the property gate that they entered and the mailman passed. Put the photos back in the plastic envelope and record who handled them.'

Morris grinned. 'Clever, Sir. I must hold them carefully then.'

Rankin said, 'After that, go out to Tedsley station and locate the people who work there and show them this picture of the bull Gardner gave me. Ask them if they had seen it as it was stolen. And establish where they were the day of the murders. The photos should be delivered to Burke as soon as possible, Take someone with you.'

The late papers and radio were informing the public that police were treating the deaths as murder-suicide, but no one knew why it had happened. It was not a big story. Rankin was grateful for that, but thought the investigation was far from complete. After supper, Rankin went to his room and Black to the bar.

The next morning, they went to the police station at ten am, sat in the incident room, and went through all statements assembled. Then they went for a long lunch and back to the station to wait for Morris to report. At four pm Morris arrived and told them the photo and prints were with Burke. He used Burke's phone to verify that the workers were at a rodeo at Longreach the weekend of the murders.

Next morning, Burke informed Rankin that the only prints in the house – on the glass and screen door – were Harvey's, his wife's and the woman who worked at the station and her prints were in the kitchen. Morris said the woman employed at the station got supplies from Tedsley Downs homestead and had stated she and Mrs Harvey always had a cup of tea in the kitchen. There were three sets of prints in the Land Rover, Harvey's, his wife and her son's.

Rankin and Black collected their luggage from the hotel office. Morris and a police constable drove them to the Winton aerodrome. Rankin gave Morris his card with all his phone numbers on it and told him to report any developments. The Dash Eight was on the tarmac, having just landed from Cloncurry. After a short flight to Emerald, they then boarded a Metro Jet back to Brisbane. Rankin spent the flight pondering the deaths.

At Brisbane airport, Rankin was met by a police car, which took him to police headquarters then continued on to take Black to his home. Back in his office, Rankin checked his in-tray, but there was nothing of real interest there. He drove his phone-equipped, private police car home. The boys gave him a boisterous welcome and Rhonda had his tea on the table. He was glad to be home.

Rankin went to his office next morning and gave his report to Wirth's secretary. After making a phone call to the uni history section, and learning a short history on what had been Ceylon, now Sri Lanka, he set up the white board, and printed the facts about the Winton events – both Burke's account of what happened, and the oddities the detectives found about his opinion.

He strolled to the bistro across the lane beside police headquarters and had a pot of tea. During the break, he thought about the Winton case, which seemed different in the cold daylight of Brisbane. Burke was probably right and it was a fact-less case.

When he got back to the office, Connors and Kennedy were examining the white board. They would soon to be joined by Black and Doyle.

He had the Ceylon photos pinned to the board; the Squad members received a short history lesson. 'Colombo was a deep water port in Ceylon, now Sri Lanka, which was once a British colony. Responding to the threat of invasion by the Japanese, many woman and their children left for safer places. That probably explained the photo of the two girls and the older boy, and where they were at the dates on the photos.

'The British had a life of ease, before the war with Japan and the threat of invasion prompted the forming of a national army by the men who stayed. Many men stayed to protect the colony but there was no invasion. After the war, their easy lifestyle was over. Ceylon nationalised their businesses, took over their exclusive clubs, and deported them. The British right-to-rule had been destroyed after the fall of Singapore.

'The fall of Singapore was a psychological blow to British expats working and living in South East Asia. The British Cruisers, Prince of Wales, and Repulse, were sunk quickly by much smaller Japanese torpedo-equipped aircraft. The British Army contingent in Singapore surrendered, outnumbering the Japanese invasion force two to one. The conquered country suffered brutal Japanese rule. The protection the British gave them was a myth. Asia did not want them back.

'Many former residents of Ceylon came to Australia because we then had a white Australian policy. If Harvey's father was one of those expats, he must have got out early, as Harvey claimed that he left him a significant legacy when he passed on.'

Rankin went to the board and commenced the sequence of events pertaining to the three Winton deaths and spoke of his concern at some aspects of the crime. The main concerns were the open fly screen door, wine as the final drink at the kitchen table when rum was available at the office desk with a more fitting chair, the pressure lamp off the table and no suicide note.

The board contained a photo of Harvey and his wife, and other photos taken from the house.

He told them that general opinion was that it was a murder and suicide, but that all people interviewed are at a loss to explain why it had happened. 'Tedsley Downs was sound financially, there was no evidence of debt, cattle gave him a good income, and his wife had inherited a business from her late husband and was well off financially. Their lives look so normal for the district. What could possibly have gone wrong?'

After considering Rankin's information, Kennedy queried, 'No photos of the two families together. Only one of Harvey with his father and sisters, and Mrs Harvey with her daughters. They were probably from different social classes.'

Doyle had been studying the board and said, 'It makes more sense if someone else killed them all.'

'Good point,' said Rankin, 'I am considering that probability, but the facts support murder-suicide. Things may be much clearer after the funerals.'

Doyle said, 'Harvey had drunk a glass and a half of wine. The lamp off the table suggests Harvey had a visitor and they had a social drink together. He and his visitor poured a glass of wine and another was poured. His visitor could have left the wine poured, made an excuse to use the sink, got the revolver, and shot Harvey in the head. Then poured his or hers glass back into the bottle and waited for Mrs Harvey to come home, killed her and her son and came back inside the house to set the scene to look like suicide. '

Kennedy smiled. 'Very fanciful. You should write penny-dreadfuls.'

Black said, 'From what we heard in Winton about the Harvey's relationship, it makes more sense than the murder-suicide theory.'

Rankin nodded. 'The senior detective at Winton has the same theory as Doyle, but on the evidence available, the coroner will bring a verdict of murder-suicide.'

After the squad meeting, Rankin rang Sloan, the estate solicitor, requesting details of the funeral arrangements. Sloan said, 'I have been in contact with all who benefit from the deceased and have been advised that Gerald Harvey is to be interned in a Melbourne cemetery next to his father, and Gwen Harvey at Parramatta in Sydney next to her first husband, the daughters' father, and her son next to her.' Rankin made a note of the addresses of Harvey's sisters and Gwen's daughters, thanked Sloan, and hung up.

The press, radio, and TV channels had wind of what happened at Winton. The apparently glamorous lifestyle of the deceased had filtered to Brisbane, and was Sunday paper fodder. Interest in the deaths was now public. The Squad knew the press would lose interest if there were no leaks. *Would Morris handle it without giving anything sensitive to them? He would,* Rankin thought.

He rang the Commissioner's office and arranged an appointment with Wirth for 11am. He took the lift to the sixth floor at 10 50 and sat in the lounge outside Wirth's office.

Wirth opened his office door and beckoned Rankin in. They sat in the small lounge in front of Wirth's desk. Wirth said, 'Problems, Vergil?'

'Something didn't add up with Winton, ' said Rankin. The Commissioner heard him out and then let out a long breath saying, 'You are drawing a long bow, Vergil.'

'Sometimes they shoot straight arrows, Sir.'

Considering the interstate implications of Rankin's request that a member of his Squad attend each funeral, Wirth warned, 'New South Wales and Victorian Police won't be happy if we leave them out of the investigation.'

Rankin said, 'We will only be paying our respects to both families, Sir. Both trips can be on private matters, but I am sure there is much to be learnt in Sydney and Melbourne.'

Wirth considered his proposal carefully. Rankin had a proven track record, but evidence to date ensured a coroner's finding of murder-suicide. Knowing it was always a gamble to back his detectives against firm evidence, Wirth said, 'Go ahead, but keep the expenses down.'

Rankin replied, 'Thanks, Sir.'

Late that afternoon, the two funeral notices and obituaries were delivered to his office. Harvey was to have a 10am service next Wednesday at a Toorak minor church. The mainstream churches would not give a service to people who suicided as they believed only God had the right to end lives. He was to be interned at a Toorak cemetery. This would be followed by a wake at a hall in Toorak.

Gwen Harvey's funeral was on the Friday of the same week. The service would be at Fairfield Catholic Church at 2pm.

The burial was to follow at Liverpool Cemetery, and the wake at the Fairfield town Hall. That gave him plenty of time to arrange things.

Connors would attend the Toorak service and wake and Rankin would attend Gwen Harvey's funeral. Arrangements were made for Rhonda to travel with Rankin to Sydney. Rhonda was excited about seeing her aunt who lived at Hornsby. She accepted Rankin's statement that he had private police business in Sydney and it would be a day trip. Neighbours would have to collect the boys after school.

He summoned Connors to his office and ran through his instructions. Connor's grammar school education and bearing would fit in with the congregation at Toorak.

Connors would fly down late afternoon, stop at the Victoria Hotel off Swanson Street, hire a car next day, locate where the funeral and wake would be held, and attend both events. Connors was told to attend the service and the internment, but not to approach the sisters until the wake. He was to introduce himself to the sisters, telling them that his uncle was a Battle for Britain pilot and he was there to pay homage to their brother, a fellow pilot, then mention that his boss at homicide was not happy with the situation at Tedsley Downs.

Rankin went on, 'Any information about the family's early life in Ceylon and after the war would be very helpful. After you state that I am not happy with the situation at Tedsley Downs, they will talk to you – particularly because you are there to honour their brother as a fighter plane pilot, as your uncle had been.'

Connors returned to his office to plan his questions and to organise his affairs in readiness for his flight the next day.

One funeral service was now covered.

Connors called at Rankin's office late that day. He had the name of his assumed uncle and details of how he was killed over France in 1940 when his Hurricane fighter plane was shot down. Kennedy, who was in Rankin's office said, 'Hurricane? I thought it was a Spitfire?'

Connors said, 'My study of the Battle for Britain concludes that the Hurricanes won it and the Spitfires cleaned up the aftermath. Harvey probably was in Legless Bader's squadron, and they flew Hurricanes.'

Details, details, Rankin chided himself for missing it.

Connors left the office and Kennedy said, 'You learn something every day.'

Everything now depended on Connors' report from Melbourne.

***

Connors rang Rankin the night of the Harvey funeral. He told him that after meeting the sisters at the wake and going through what he had been told to do, he had their attention for much of the wake.

The sisters told Connors that they had been deported from Ceylon after the war when the new government nationalised all foreign business and they left penniless. The Harvey family came to Australia because of its white Australia policy.

One of them told Connors, 'Daddy got a job as an accountant with one of the other expats, but we lived close to the bone in the awful suburb of Surry Hills. Mother died two years later. Gerald was reduced to giving joy-flights out of a Sydney air field. But he had incredible luck and won a major jackpot at the races. The jackpot required him to pick the winners of seven races. It paid a hundred and twenty-five thousand pounds. He gave Father thirty thousand pounds and my sister and I twenty thousand each.

'We could at last live in a decent suburb and be members of the correct social clubs. Melbourne with its Englishness beckoned. We became members of the Athena Club; Daddy was accepted into the Melbourne Club. We found suitable husbands and Daddy now had his own accountancy practice. He passed away two years later and we inherited his wealth. He and Mother could not accept what had happened to them – reduced to not having a cleaning woman. Mummy had to do the cooking and clean the house at Surry Hills and we had to make out own beds. In Ceylon, we had many servants to do this.'

Connors asked Harvey's sisters for cards to keep in touch with them and they opened hand bags, which had a wallet of cards in them. He noticed an ANZ bankcard in one of them. Gwen's family was not represented at Harvey's funeral.

Rankin thanked him for a job well done and sat sifting Connors information through his brain. This did not add up, made no sense at all.

Something was odd here. Harvey did not inherit money from his father's death, as stated by Bowden, the bank manager at Winton. But maybe he lied to the bank manager because he thought that was better than admitting it was the proceeds of gambling. When he deducted the money given to his family from the hundred and twenty-five thousand pounds he won what he arrived with at Winton left only five thousand pounds unaccounted for. Probably expense money.

A telephone call to the local TAB administration office produced information about how big wins were paid out. Payments were made mainly by cheque, the ticket holder was entitled to cash if demanded and prepared to wait for his money. He asked about a big Sydney jackpot about eleven years ago and the clerk said he would get back to him.

Ten minutes later the clerk phoned Rankin advising that there had been a record jackpot in Sydney at their winter carnival years ago. It required picking seven straight winners. Three ticket holders had collected over a hundred and twenty-five thousand pounds, but that was a oncer over the winter carnival races eleven years ago. No record was kept on who they were and most big winners kept it to themselves, as there would people wanting a handout. Rankin thanked him, noting the date of the payout.

Next, he made a telephone call to the ANZ bank at Toorak. Identifying himself, Rankin asked to speak to the manager. He was put through to him and asked him if the Harvey sisters had bank accounts with his bank before they were married, and if they had, what was the date that twenty thousand pounds was deposited in their accounts, and was it cheque or cash. The manager said he could not divulge and information on bank clients. Rankin told him that if he was not forthcoming with the information, Victorian police would be requested to seize their records.

The manager said he would ring him back. Rankin had to wait fifteen minutes before the manager called back. He gave Rankin a date and said the deposits were bank cheques and paid into their newly opened accounts. The sisters had told him their brother Gerald had a big win at the races. 'Terrible business, what happened to him,' he said.

Rankin said, 'To the three of them.'

The manager said, 'This will go no further.'

Rankin now had the dates of the race jackpot and the sums of money Harvey gave to his sisters. It married up. There were ten days between the race and the deposits, in the correct order. He had a busy morning preparing for his and Rhonda's trip to Sydney.

After a late lunch at the popular local bistro, he analysed the information he had. Harvey had lied to the bank manager at Winton about the source of his money, but that appeared irrelevant to his murder. That he was hiding from someone or something was negated by his open lifestyle.

After lunch, Rankin was joined by his squad at his office, all eager to hear the results of Connor's day in Melbourne.

The next day, Rankin and his wife flew to Sydney, hired a car at Sydney airport, and went to his wife's aunt's house.

He then went on to Mascot airport to attend a pre-arranged interview with the aero club secretary. She confirmed Gerald Harvey had once been a member of the club – long before her time. She thought that two long-term employees might be able to assist Rankin with his inquiries.

Barney Miller and Howard Day walked out from the aircraft hangar to meet Rankin and his escort. After the introductions were made, Rankin mentioned his interest in Gerald Harvey. He was surprised to find that both men were aware of Harvey's death. *Small world,* thought Rankin.

When asked for their opinions, Barney replied, 'Cold and reserved, but never condescending or sarcastic like some of the Poms were.' Howard continued, 'We met Harvey during the war; serviced his Hurricane.'

Intrigued, Rankin asked, 'You knew him well?'

Howie replied, 'No one knew Harvey well. Cold and unapproachable – just a kid then. Great fighter pilot, brave and deadly. Most of the squadron had great respect for him but he never socialised with them.' Holding their interest Rankin casually asked about the winnings at the races.

Howie replied, 'Over a hundred thousand quid. Sent two hundred to the club to buy drinks.' Barney quietly said, 'Post war trauma – it gets a lot of them. They carry their own dead without remorse, but the people they killed come back to haunt them.'

Rankin thanked them and he left. He thought post war trauma would be another reason for the Coroner to give a murder-suicide finding, Harvey could have been suffering from it.

After a quick lunch, Rankin drove to Fairfield to locate the church and hall in which the wake would be held. He joined a slow moving funeral crowd, and settled into a seat behind the grieving family members in the front rows on the left hand side of the church. Two coffins rested in front of the altar.

The family consisted of two women wearing black dresses, accompanied by two large men in black suits – Gwen Harvey's daughters and their husbands. Rankin knew their names from the funeral notices, but didn't know who was who. Seven children occupied the seats behind the two daughters and their husbands.

From the funeral notices, he knew the daughters were Betty Clifford and her husband, Dane and Silvia Roberts and her husband, Clive.

The murdered son was Steven Springfield, the young brother of the women. A priest came from behind the altar at the back of the building; everyone rose as he entered. He was a big man, round-faced with short greying hair. The order of service said he was Father Manning.

The funeral service commenced. The priest said, 'Be seated,' in measured tones. Father Manning gave a brief speech about Gwen and her generosity to her family and the sad way she and her son Steven died. He then said, 'Let us pray for their souls to be released from purgatory and join God in heaven.' The congregation knelt, except the elderly who remained seated. After the prayers, the congregation were seated. Two daughters went to a raised platform with a microphone.

Betty gave the eulogy, both sisters were tearful and supporting each other. The Order of Service pictured Gwen and Steven on the front page. After Betty had finished, the two tearful women returned to their seats to be comforted by the men. Rankin now knew who was married to whom.

The priest immediately asked them to pray, cutting off any maudlin speeches. He would say the long prayer at the internment and confined his prayer now to the confidia dao in Latin. The song, 'Somewhere Over The Rainbow' came through the speakers as the coffins were wheeled out of the church. The daughters and families followed behind. Steven's coffin was lifted into the black hearse by the young people, whilst Gwen's coffin was lifted by Dane and Clive with assistance from family friends.

After allowing time for a smoke, which most men enjoyed, the funeral cortege moved off with the daughters and their husbands in the front car and older women and youths in the second. They were followed by a long procession of cars to the Liverpool cemetery. The children did not attend the internment.

Rankin did not go to the internment, but went to his car and drove to Fairfield Town Hall ready to join the family at the wake. As was the case with Gerald Harvey's funeral, no in-laws attended Gwen's funeral.

He sat thinking about what he had learnt. Harvey was definitely a fighter pilot in the Battle of Britain, according to the flight riggers, who Rankin believed.

Their profile of Harvey fitted with what we know of him from Winton, and they confirmed he won the jackpot at the races. There was hardly a mention of their brother Steven in Betty's eulogy. Odd. Very odd. They were siblings after all. This boy, Steven seemed not to have rated in the family.

Hopefully, loose conversations at the wake may throw some light on this family. The dynamics of the family were hazy at best. Inside the hall, long tables of food had been set up, with chairs along both sides for those who preferred to sit. Cold drinks and beer were freely available. The people returned from the interment. There was much to talk about after this funeral. Everyone was curious. Rankin heard people wondering aloud about what had really happened at Tedsley Downs. From overheard conversations, it seemed Gwen had seemed content in her letters to family and friends. Now, Rankin was curious too.

The sisters arrived and people were coming up to them, cuddling them, and kissing their cheeks. Clive and Dane were at a table with a number of large men tossing down beers. Waiting until this died off, Rankin then joined the sisters. He introduced himself, and said that he was in Sydney on another matter, but had felt obliged to pay his respects as the three deaths were still under investigation.

The woman again burst into tears. Clive joined them. Glaring at Rankin, in a firm voice, Clive asked, 'What was going on?'

Rankin introduced himself to him. Seeing the newcomer, Dane moved to his wife's side, joining the group.

Rankin said, 'From all reports in Winton, your mother was very well liked and previously a business woman.'

Slightly hot under the collar, Clive spat out, 'That sounds better than billiard saloon keeper and SP bookie.' Silvia glared at Clive and said, 'She was good to you.' Cooling, Clive replied, 'I meant no offence. I loved your mother, but all of this is getting to me – the murder of your mother, today, and now him.' He pointed at Rankin. Clive continued, 'She was never charged with any offence and paid you blokes plenty to avoid it.'

Silvia stepped up, 'Mum was a lady, but could be as tough as nails if necessary.'

In a conciliatory tone, Rankin murmured, 'It must be hard coming to terms with happened. The loss of a mother and brother.'

Clive looked straight at Rankin. 'Steven was no loss!'

Betty, quiet until now, joined the fray. 'You should not speak ill of the dead.'

Her husband, Dane, watchful up until now, said in low tones, 'He was a creep who fiddled with our daughters.'

Clive exploded. 'And our boys. And you had the evidence to do something about it, Betty, and did nothing.'

Betty, now fully composed rose to the occasion. 'Mother said she would take Steven to Tedsley Downs station, and get him out of everyone's way.'

Now Silvia turned to Betty, red-faced. 'And you let her stop you from reporting the little creep.' Defending her late mother, Silvia replied, 'We all owe her. She gave us the deposits for our homes.' Things were getting out of hand with this family, but Rankin made himself invisible as the storm brewed and Clive replied, 'And we all paid her back.'

Betty said, 'So we should have.'

On leaving the family group to their anger, Rankin thought, 'Why would a happy couple end up as they did?'

Hoping for more background on the family, Rankin asked Father Manning for his insight. 'I married the Harveys. He would not become a Catholic, but agreed to any children borne of the union being brought up Catholics, as unlikely as it seemed that they would have children. I married both of her daughters. Steven, her son, was unmarried.'

Continuing he said, 'Steven didn't fit in with the families. He lived with both his sisters and his mother as the mood took him. He would not work and lived on welfare and money from his mother. Their husbands detested him.'

Rankin asked, 'Did Harvey have much contact with the families?'

Father Manning replied, 'The Harveys always came down for the Royal Easter Show. Gwen spent time with both her daughters. Gerald paid his respects, but stayed in town at a city hotel.'

Rankin said, 'No one from Harvey's family appeared to be at the service.'

The priest said, 'They didn't mix. Sorry, I must be off. Rosary and Benediction at the church tonight.'

Rankin observed in passing, 'The girls married big men.'

The priest said, 'Both front row forwards in our local union team. The full scrum is here. They play together when work allows it. Clive is a railway engine driver and Dane a fireman. Both are good husbands and have happy marriages.'

Rankin said, 'Betty's mother had a big influence on her.'

The priest said, 'Betty was slow to mature and needed her mother's guidance until she was married.'

The priest then hurried off to Betty and Silvia, had a brief word with them, and left. Rankin went to the husbands and got Dane's eye.

Rankin said, 'Did the boy fiddle with any of your team mate's children?'

Choosing his words carefully Dane replied, 'Yes, when we went out as a group, he always minded the children for us. We trusted the little creep.' Dane paused then said, 'But the only one who caught him in the act was Betty and she wouldn't report him. Allegations from young children are often dismissed.'

Rankin left him and drove to join Rhonda at her aunt's house at Hornsby. He apologised to the aunt for the short visit and he and Rhonda left for the airport, returned the hire car, and flew home.

Rankin was at his office next morning, Saturday.

Rhonda was not happy with him as both boys were playing soccer that morning and wanted him to be there but he wanted to be alone at his office. He needed to analyse what had been learnt in Melbourne and Sydney and draft his report for Wirth. Mrs Harvey had daughters with working husbands, and they were full time mothers. The refusal of Betty to have her brother reported and properly assessed by a mental health specialist, despite the wishes of her husband and her sister and her husband, was odd as he was only a fiddler, but could have matured into a serious sexual offender.

Her domination by her mother was odd under the circumstances. But the young paedophile had fiddled with many children and gone unreported. He was sent to Winton to join his mother. Why was his mother so mentally absent regarding her son? This secret died with Gwen.

He went home for lunch and to excited sons telling him about the game, and a silent, miffed wife. After lunch, the boys went down at the local milk bar, their hangout, and his wife visited friends. He lay on the long lounge and slept. He had done everything possible for the moment.

Sunday, he took the boys and his wife to the north coast – everyone had an enjoyable day. That night after the boys went to bed and TV was finished, he and his wife went to bed. When he reached for her, she came to him willingly.

Monday at his office, after he and his team went through what he had learnt in Sydney, and Connors in Melbourne, he sent his report up to Wirth's office.

He asked the team for observations. Kennedy said, 'Gerald Harvey lied to the Winton bank about his source of the money he deposited with them, but that has no bearing on his murdering his wife and son and his suicide.'

Rankin nodded, 'I agree. Regardless of the oddities of his wealth, I don't think it has any bearing on the Tedsley Downs Station killings. Mrs Harvey's son being a sexual fiddler is interesting, as is the mother of a victim's reluctance to do anything about it, and the influence of Mrs Harvey in that decision.'

Kennedy, ever the pragmatist, said, 'Not really – keep it in the family.'

Black said, 'Yeah, it's a bit odd. The father of the girls and boys fiddled with and Betty's sister wanted him reported, but Betty, who could have brought a case against him, wouldn't because of her mother. So we have a young paedophile among the murder victims. A mother and her deviate son murdered and the woman's husband suiciding after killing them.'

'That's what the Coroner will decide, but I am not completely happy with it,' Rankin replied.

Connors said, 'The husbands had a motive to kill Steven.'

Rankin nodded. 'But I have established their whereabouts at the time of the murders; Clive was driving a train the Friday of the crime and Dane was on duty at the Parramatta fire service. But they are not the only ones involved. A number of other families had young children who were fiddled with.'

Later, he attended a meeting with Commissioner Wirth who had studied the report. He said, 'Interesting, Vergil, but it doesn't alter the murder-suicide. The Coroner will find on the evidence presented. Anything outside of that is irrelevant. Close the case and get on with other work.'

Frustrated, Rankin said, 'With respect, Sir, there are a number of people outside the family whose children were victims of the young paedophile. There is plenty of motive for revenge against Steven. I would like an investigation of all parents and their whereabouts at the time of the murders.'

Wirth said, 'New South Wales police would have to handle it. I will take the necessary steps and you will be kept in the picture.'

The Coroner made a finding of murder-suicide on the Tedsley Downs killings, but Rankin believed the case was not closed.

CHAPTER 6

GREEK MURDER MACKAY

The old Greek heard the knocking on the back door of the café where he lived in a small, dingy flat. Cautiously, he opened the back door. A shotgun blast hit him in the chest, knocking him awkwardly off his feet. He collapsed onto the drab lino floor.

A neighbour heard the explosion and rushed to the old man's back door. In shock and disbelief, he slowly staggered back into the yard, barely holding back vomit that was quickly rising in his throat. Slightly recovering, adrenalin kicked in. He took in the sight of the old man's body with a blasted gaping wound. Blood was now slowly bubbling out of what was left of the chest and silver coins were tossed over the body. He could not believe the sight in front of him.

Others had now joined him. Phone calls were urgently made to the ambulance and to the police. *How did this happen on a quiet Sunday night?* they all wondered.

The patrolling police were soon at the scene. They taped it off and waited for the CIB and forensic divisions, which took time to muster late Sunday night. The murdered man was Cornelius Comino. His son, Viktor, owned the café.

Cornelius, a widower, helped around the busy café, acting as caretaker when the business was closed.

The police officers studied the scene. The bloody body lay on the floor at the back door of the cafe, a sawn off shotgun dumped at the doorway. Several silver coins had been thrown on the body, decorating it like an offering.

Local police were at a loss to understand the killing, as the old man was harmless and as far as could be established, had no enemies.

His son, Viktor Comino, was a business man, self-made and a known hard business man. He was married and had two girls at boarding school. He was said to be a womaniser.

Steele, the senior detective based at Mackay, supported by a big uniformed presence, made no real progress with the investigation. No motive, no eyewitnesses.

Steele pondered the evidence to hand. The thirty silver coins denoted a traitor, a Judas in the Old Testament. So they were looking for a killer with a sense of history and knowledge of the Bible, so not a member of the younger generation. They were not interested in tales of the Bible. And an elderly Greek victim was unusual. The Greeks always floated in the background. They knew their place in this country. Didn't they? He knew he couldn't expect much help from the local Greeks, they close ranks – old country habits die hard, even after a generation in their new country.

Steele believed it could be over something in the past, maybe the long distant past; the victim would in his seventies. His investigation of the Comino family had revealed Viktor, his brother Theodora' and his sister Largo, had been brought out from Greece by an uncle.

They had been put to work to pay back their fare on very low money and long working hours.

Viktor had teamed up with an old Greek who had paid the money owing on his sponsored fare and made Viktor a partner in the business, to avoid paying wages. Viktor walked into a run-down Greek café. The old Greek was too mean to spend money on the premises or pay staff a living wage.

With youth and showmanship, Viktor built a thriving business. After many arguments, he bought out the old Greek, and paid out the remainder of the debts owed by his brother and his sister to the sponsor. The family worked hard in the café and they all prospered.

Cornelius had lived with his wife, who had now pre-deceased him, in the large Greek city of Patros east of Athens. Her dying wish was to be buried in Athens where they both came from, and wished a full Greek Orthodox Church funeral service.

Viktor, his brother and sister travelled to Greece for the traditional Orthodox funeral. Following the funeral, Cornelius was persuaded to join his children in Australia. This was the future. Greece was politically unstable and broke. Life went on for them all. Their father was now a victim of a shotgun blast, and a message was left by the thirty pieces of silver. A message to whom? A message from whom?

The shotgun, casually left at the murder scene held no clues; it was old and there was no requirement to register guns in this state or record who bought it.

The police investigation meandered on in Mackay. No calls from the public. The local Greek community was reticent to say anything.

Then, out of the blue, another old Greek was murdered with a shotgun at Rockhampton a fortnight later. Silver coins were thrown over his body and a sawn off shotgun left at the scene. Queensland's State Homicide Squad was quickly appointed to investigate both murders.

Chief Inspector Virgil Rankin and Detective Doyle flew to Mackay and Detective Sergeants Kennedy, Black, and Connors travelled to Rockhampton to assist the local CIB.

At Mackay Police Headquarters, Steele brought Rankin up-to-date on the known facts of the murder and the victim. They had found no known motive for the old man's death, no eyewitnesses to the crime. Greeks were part of the community, owning the Cafes and fast food outlets. Steele had learnt the family history from other local Greeks who his team had questioned during their investigation.

Steele, together with Rankin's team inspected the murder scene, studying the police photos of the body. The thirty silver coins were of interest, as was the weapon used.

Rankin and Steele agreed the father's murder could have been over something that had happened in the past or a warning to someone. The Greek community in Mackay had been crime free in living memory, but Viktor had a reputation for sailing close to the wind.

An incident board was set up at the Mackay Police Headquarters recording all known information.

137

Rankin asked, 'Any old Greeks that we can talk to about their home country customs?'

Steele replied, 'Collardi, he owns a picture show business, and owes me a favour.'

Steele and Rankin drove to the old picture show building. Poorly maintained, it had probably seen better days.

Drive-in movies had made theatres outdated. After introductions were made, Rankin said to Collardi, 'You would be aware of Cornelius Comino's death; what is your opinion of the method used, and the thirty pieces of silver thrown on his body?'

Collardi replied in very poor English, 'Mr Policeman, I did not know Cornelius before he came here. We played cards and other games together with other old Greeks. We did not talk about the old days in Greece. When Germany invaded Greece, there was much bloodshed. We fought the German army for two hundred and nineteen days; a professional army, they were too strong for us. We were amateurs fighting for our homes.

'The Germans rounded up all Jews from our villages, trucked them in open train wagons to Poland where most of them were sent to the gas chambers; very few survived to come back to Greece. Their businesses became German property. They were given to Greeks who informed on the Jews and on our underground resistance. Their reward was a good Jewish business. Like all conquered countries, there are always people who will betray their own and side with the invader. Cornelius arrived here poor and dependent on his son Viktor for his upkeep. I believe his killing was not by a local. It must be for something in the past. But why? He was a very old man.'

Greek revenge thought Rankin – or Jewish. Greeks and Jews are an unforgiving mob. There is no time limit on their revenge for traitors. Jews are better organized and good at assassination, but the weapon used was in the Greek tradition. The reported thirty silver coins denoted a traitor, a Judas.

Rankin thanked the old picture show man. Back at Mackay Police Headquarters, it was hard to know how to update the incident board. A real can of worms. He rang the Rockhampton police headquarters leaving a message for Kennedy to ring him.

It was time to meet Viktor. Rankin and Burgess, Steele's second-in-command, drove to a modern warehouse located in an old residential suburb of Mackay. Viktor was supervising two men unloading a truck.

Viktor strode over to them saying, 'Police,' before Rankin could produce his badge.

Rankin nodded and Viktor said aggressively, 'What are you doing about catching the person who murdered my father?'

Rankin replied, 'Everything possible.'

'Not good enough, he was murdered over a fortnight ago and his killer should be behind bars by now … if you were doing your job.'

Rankin let the remark go through to the keeper and said, 'What did your father do in Greece?'

'What's that got to do with anything?' said Viktor.

Rankin's eyes narrowed. 'Just answer the question.'

Viktor said, 'He was a business man in Athens before the Germans came. They took his building and stock.

139

'He worked on a fishing boat owned by the Germans during the occupation. After the war, he moved the family to Patras as Greece was in a state of turmoil. He worked as labourer at any job he could get to support my mother and our family. He got a sponsor to get my brother, my sister, and me to Australia as DPs.

'My mother took us to Athens as DP, displaced persons, and from there we got to here. Australia was looking for immigrants as long as they were European, that requirement later extended to Mediterranean races. I was fifteen, and had to work out a debt on very low wages to the Greek who sponsored me – as had my brother and sister. That would have taken years. An old Greek had a rundown café.

'I put a business deal to the owner to pay the amount owed to the sponsor and I would work for him as a junior partner. Two years later, I bought him out. It was by then a thriving business, which I had built up by working long hours.'

Rankin said, 'You came here as an economic slave?'

Viktor sneered, 'We knew no better and were threatened with deportment if we misbehaved. We did not then speak English; it was how it was then. Now, get on with finding my father's killer.'

Viktor turned his back on the detectives and returned to what he was doing. Burgess went to say something, but quickly, Rankin stopped him. They returned to their car. Burgess said, 'Arrogant wog. You should have slapped him down.'

Rankin said, 'There could be another meeting with him, but if he continues the way he did, we will handle him. We now have a reverse statement of what I perceived to have happened in war-time Greece.'

Back at the police station, Rankin updated his incident board. No real progress had been made, but it was only day one for the Homicide Squad.

Rankin and Doyle went back to see the picture show owner, Collardi. Rankin said to him, 'Viktor's father was in Athens during the war, but shifted to a busy city after the war.'

Collardi said, 'Many Greeks left Athens after the war for a number of reasons. The Germans destroyed a lot of identity papers and after the war, many Greeks were DP.'

Rankin said, 'Some were German collaborators?'

Collardi said, 'Yes, and some left to escape the troubles in Greece.'

Rankin said, 'Victor stated that his mother arranged for his passage to Australia. I find that strange. It would be a long trip to Athens for a woman and three children alone.'

Collardi said, 'That is strange, but there must have been a reason. Things were different then, post war.'

Rankin said, 'A man wanted for collaborating with the Germans would not want to leave a place he considered was safe.'

Flustered, Collardi said, 'Mr Policeman, rumour can spread like a bag of feathers in the wind and it often harms the innocent as well as the guilty. The past is gone and many things best left alone.'

The detectives thanked the old man and returned to the car. In the car Rankin said, 'I believe the father was murdered for something in the past. He surfaced at his wife's funeral, someone arranged for him to obtain papers to come to Australia. Maybe that alerted someone looking for traitors.'

Kennedy rang Rankin from Rockhampton. After an examination of the known facts of the Rockhampton murder, significant differences existed between the Greeks murdered. The Mackay Greek was poor and dependant – Theodorus, the murdered Rockhampton Greek was wealthy. The Mackay Greek was from Greece – Theodorus from Cyprus.

Rankin had a meeting with Steele and Burgess at the police station. They all agreed the investigation had bogged down. Rankin stated more might be learnt in Rockhampton and that he and Doyle would fly there this afternoon.

CHAPTER 7

GREEK MURDERS ROCKHAMPTON

Kennedy collected Rankin and Doyle at Rockhampton Airport and on the drive to police headquarters, brought him up to date on their inquiry.

Rockhampton CIB Chief, Backhouse, and his deputy, Johnson, had supervised a thorough investigation of the Greek murder. They had taken a suspect into custody, but had released him after a long questioning. They spoke of the significant differences between the Rockhampton and Mackay Greek murders – the different place of origin and status.

But many things were the same. The silver coins were the same denomination in both cases. Both men were killed by a shotgun blast on a Sunday night in a regional town. In both cases, the sawn off shotgun was casually dropped at the site. Both bodies had thirty silver coins thrown on them, the price of a Judas, a traitor. This much he knew from Kennedy's phone call a few days ago. Rankin was beginning to think the setting of the second scene by the murderer was a copycat killing, but the coins used in both cases were the same denomination and so connected them.

At Rockhampton Police Headquarters, Rankin paid his respects to the area superintendent, Burton, and went to the incident room set up by Backhouse.

He studied the information on Theodorus. He, his wife, and their five children had left Cyprus during the civil unrest that shook Cyprus after the second world war. With many other Cypriots the family escaped to Israel and then to Australia, settling in Rockhampton.

With funds smuggled from Cyprus, Theodorus purchased a fruit and vegetable business. With hard work and long hours and all the family working in the business, he became very wealthy. He owned three cafes, an impressive fruit market, together with a spread of properties, accumulated over his thirty years here. He was semi-retired at age seventy and living quietly within the Greek community. Now a widower, he had some of his adult children living around him. *A good life, well lived. A violent death. Nothing made sense,* Rankin thought.

Rankin studied the incident board previously prepared by Backhouse. Theodorus had been gunned down at the large modern home unit in which he had lived. A shotgun was the weapon used, as was the case in Mackay. A security guard been the first on the scene and had rung the police.

Theodorus had two sons, three daughters, and eleven grandchildren. The daughters had married Australian Greek men. One daughter was divorced from her husband and was living with a man in a defacto relationship. He was the security guard who had found Theodorus during his evening rounds.

The men who had married his daughters worked for him. His girls had a basic education, as Greek women were expected to be married, bear children, and become full time mothers.

His two sons had attended good colleges and were now barristers in Brisbane. His daughters were now full time mothers, except for the youngest daughter Marree, who had married at age twenty, had two children, and divorced her Greek husband, Condarus. He was rearing their children with the help of a live-in housekeeper. The divorced husband now managed Arron Theodorus' biggest café restaurant called The New World. It is located in one of the main streets of the CBD with hotels on each corner opposite.

Marree, now aged thirty-two had a police record for drunken behaviour, resisting arrest, causing trouble in hotels, and being a public nuisance. Theodorus had disowned her. Condarus had been granted custody of the children. She was now on a two year good behaviour bond. Her defacto husband was older than she was and had settled her down.

Kennedy, Connors, Black, and Doyle had now assembled at Rockhampton police headquarters casually comparing notes. Backhouse, the head detective in the area, and his second-in-command, Johnson were absent. The Greek factor made things interesting. They all finished at five pm and went to their hotel on the riverbank, settling in at the bar after dinner. Rankin, a non-drinker, went to his room and rang Commissioner Wirth to give him a preliminary view based on the information collated on the incident board. Lastly, before sleep, he made a quick call home to his wife, Rhonda.

At the joint squads meeting the next day, Backhouse gave a summary of his team's investigation and the release of the security guard, Simon Blake.

Essentially, Blake had gone into the large unit block that Arron Theodorus owned and entered a ground floor garden unit where he lived. The large family house had been sold after he was widowed. The firm Blake worked for had the security contract on the building. Blake stated he had entered the unit block grounds after ringing his firm's office at eleven o'clock for his hourly report, as required. He had checked the front and garage area of the unit block and had lodged his card in the slot on the side wall near the fuse boxes, at the entrance to the unit complex. The card recorded the time of his visit.

Just as he was leaving, Blake had heard the loud explosion of a heavy weapon being fired nearby. Blake drew his revolver and ran to the front of the building where he thought the noise had come from. A porch light was now on. The porch had been in darkness when Blake had passed a few minutes earlier.

Within seconds, Blake was stopped in his tracks by the sight of what remained of the torso of Arron Theodorus slumped on the marble floor just inside his unit, a shotgun dumped in the doorway. Blake could see that Theodorus was beyond help. He broke open the gun to ensure it had fired both barrels. It was only then that Blake noticed pieces of what looked like silver.

His training kicked in. He made an immediate call to the police. Two patrol constables arrived and taped off the area. Both were white-faced and one sick when they saw Theodorus' mutilated body.

Johnson was the first CIB man to the scene. Blake was taken to police headquarters.

Gun residue was on his hands, his finger prints were on the murder weapon, and blood was on the soles of his shoes. But the time between when he logged into his office on the hour, went around the building, put his card in the slot, and rang the police did not allow him time to kill Theodorus.

A tenant above Theodorus' unit had seen Blake coming past her unit from the end of the building where he logged his time card. She saw him run to where Theodorus lay after the gun blast. Johnson noted that Blake had seemed calm and unaffected by what happened, and asked him about this. Blake replied that he had served in Korea in the armed forces, but did not enlarge on it. His statement of events was checked and established to be correct.

They established that Blake would not have had the time to kill Theodorus and had no motive. There were no eyewitnesses to the shooting. His prints on the shotgun were only where he said he opened the weapon and the blood on his shoe soles from inspecting the victim.

Rankin commenced to write on a fresh whiteboard. Names of victims: Arron Theodorus and Cornelius Comonio, both Greeks but from different countries. Both murdered with shotguns, on a Sunday night and both had the thirty pieces of silver thrown over the dead bodies.

Rumours floated around about the Mackay victim, Cornelius Comonio's past but they were only conjecture – nothing about the past life of Theodorus in Cyprus stood out.

Leading off the discussion, Rankin said, 'I believe they are unrelated murders. This Rockhampton murder is a copycat to confuse us, but let's keep an open mind at all times. Any opinions?'

Johnson kicked things off. 'The coins are the same denomination and must connect them. I'm not convinced they are not connected.'

Rankin said, 'Good point, but Viktor Comonio would have had calls of condolence from many Greeks and he could have mentioned this.'

Ever the pragmatist, Black took another tack, 'We need to know who benefits from Theodorus' death.'

Rankin agreed and Backhouse said, 'We will be seeing his solicitor this morning.' To everyone's surprise Rankin over-ruled Backhouse, stating that he and Kennedy would keep the appointment with the solicitor. Backhouse went bright red and had trouble containing his anger at being dismissed by Rankin.

Connors, Black, and Doyle were left to go through all statements on file. Perhaps something had been overlooked by the locals.

Recovering his ground, Backhouse said, 'We have another local murder to investigate. A man was garrotted in a riverbank public parking area the Friday before Theodorus was murdered. All available officers have been working on both cases.' He and Johnson left. 'Not a happy man,' bemused Connors.

At 10am, Rankin and Kennedy were shown to the senior solicitor's office.

Bowman, the senior partner, a small grey-haired man, got straight to the point.

'You are here to find out who benefits from Arron Theodorus' death. His will is simple. His whole estate is to go to his family, except legacies to Marree's children. They are to be managed by his sons until the youngest reaches maturity at age twenty-one. The balance of his estate will be shared equally among his adult children.'

All this sounded very fair but not consistent with police information. 'We have been informed that his daughter Marree was disowned by him.'

Nonplussed, Bowman replied, 'That is the terms of the will. His sons and I will have a meeting to decide on the best way of honouring his wishes. The estate will attract death duties, but insurance on him, paid by his sons will cover that and leave a large estate.

'When his wife died, a codicil was added to his will leaving a legacy to Marree's two children with a vesting age of twenty one and his sons as trustees. We are waiting for his death certificate to be issued and will then carry out his wishes. Arron's interment will be in two weeks to allow overseas relations to attend the service and wake.' Bowman rose, the meeting over as far as he was concerned.

Ignoring Bowman's move, Rankin continued, 'More questions, Mr Bowman. Could any beneficiary have knowledge of the will's contents?'

Confidently Bowman replied, 'Not unless Arron told them.'

'Could anyone in your firm have disclosed the contents to anyone?'

Bowman sat back in his chair, took a deep breath, and said, 'Wills are kept in a locked safe, and there are only three keys to it. Myself, and two senior partners have them.'

Rankin, not believing this, continued, 'And only you and your partners open the safe.'

Eyes narrowed in annoyance, Bowman snapped, 'Senior staff is given the keys to find documents as needed, no one else.'

Kennedy asked, 'Would witnesses to the will have a knowledge of the document's contents?'

Bowman shook his head and sighed. 'No, they can only witness signatures.'

Finally, Rankin asked Bowman, 'Where are the keys kept?'

'Locked in our office desks.'

Rankin thanked him and they left.

'Born to rule, the old bugger,' said Kennedy.

Local police had accumulated information on the victim and his family from the other people living in the unit block. They received not of much value. They said they mostly kept to themselves.

The murder had happened around 11pm. Police had established that Arron had been at a family gathering at the home of one of his married daughters that night. He left in his car at about 10.40pm.

His in-laws supplied alibis for each other's whereabouts when Arron was killed. Condarus, the divorced son-in-law, left the gathering alone, about ten minutes after Theodorus.

But his housekeeper said he was home at 11pm. She was awake and heard the hour clock in his office chiming when he entered the house. She said she always heard Mr Condarus arrive home. He had a Peugeot diesel that had to be let run for a time after stopping. That would mean he was home ten minutes after he left the family group.

Rankin though that if the guard, Simon Blake, and Marree knew the will's contents, they had motive to kill Arron. Marree was a big winner from his death. But some local, inside knowledge was needed to access the terms of the will.

Backhouse had previously told the team that Simon Blake, the security guard was not known to local police – however, Marree's police record was well known.

Kennedy had established that all members of his family and extended family were upper-middle-class and appeared financially sound – with the obvious exception of Marree. She had motive, her defacto husband had the opportunity; but would they have known the contents of Arron's will?

Bowman was clear that no one was aware of the terms of the will, not even the victim's solicitor sons. The only contact his legal firm had with Marree was a court appearance on her behalf by one of the firm's very junior solicitors.

Rankin wrote on the incident board; Main Beneficiaries from the murder, Sons, daughters, sons-in-laws, because their wives would give their share to their husbands under Greek tradition, and Marree and her two children.

Extended family history: complete investigation into them required.

Blake, the security man: history: ex-military, employed by same firm for five years. His boss stated he was a sober, reliable, stable bloke. The only hobby Blake had was fishing for mackerel off the coast. He owned a share in a boat and a share in a local race horse. He attended local race meetings with Marree, but neither were noticeable punters. They just enjoyed the atmosphere.

Blake's schedule for the day had been requested from his boss. The owner, West, said it was payroll day and Blake was working with two others in an armoured van. The run would be completed at around four pm. Rankin asked West to keep Blake there if they finished early.

At four pm, Rankin and Black were shown to a small back office, full of clutter, at West's security firm. Standing behind a desk was a tall, solid man, balding, aged about in his forties. His stance said, don't mess with me. Rankin showed his badge saying, 'Mr Blake, you would know why I am here.'

Blake replied, 'I have given statements to the local police and been questioned by detectives Backhouse and Johnson; I have nothing more to add.'

Rankin said, 'You and Marree Theodorus have a relationship. Do you expect a part of Theo's wealth?'

Simon Blake looked at Rankin and said, 'Marree and her father did not speak. He and the family disowned her. She expects nothing and will get nothing.'

Rankin tried another tack, 'Your statement of events surrounding Arron Theodorus's murder is firm, and you have nothing to add to it?'

Blake replied, 'No.'

Undeterred, Rankin continued, 'Did you hear any traffic around the road past the unit?'

Blake replied, 'After finding the body, I went through standard procedure. I am slightly hard of hearing and the shotgun blast affected my ears. There is always some traffic in the area. I have told you all I know and that's it.'

Rankin nodded and thanked him. He and Black left the security premises; Blake remained in the office.

Out of earshot, Black said, 'Hard man.' Back at the police station, Connors was instructed to keep Marree under observation. Her habits were known so not a difficult task. When Blake was on day work, Marree hung out in the city at a pub in the main street; ate free-of-charge at her father's New World Café Restaurant managed by her ex-husband Gorgio Condarus. She went home when Blake finished work. When he was on night shift, she shopped locally but was mainly home. She was barred at her local pub, which she lived opposite. Rankin told Connors to keep Marree under observation from today and to interview her neighbours.

Wearing casual clothes, carrying a large clip board, and carrying an electoral roll badge, Connors was a natural, chatting with those at home who were happy to confirm their names, which were on the roll. People like to gossip.

Backhouse had interviewed Marree, but Kennedy reinterviewed her. Rankin read the reports.

Marree appeared dismayed at what happened to her father and could not understand it. She was with friends when he was killed and that was verified.

Back at the police station, Rankin was keen to hear any personal observations. Kennedy said, 'She was once a head-turner, but her lifestyle is starting to affect her looks, and body. But she is holding up well.'

The team went to their riverbank hotel at the end of a busy day and waited for the dining room to open. Connors had reported that Marree's neighbours hardly knew Marree. She was not a church attendee, as most of them were, and not on any school committees. They said she and an older man lived quietly in their house, but they had heard things about her.

Connors remained on the surveillance until Blake came home. Marree had spent the day at home. Rankin told him to continue the surveillance tomorrow.

Johnson and Backhouse declined to join the Brisbane detectives for a meal. They were too busy handling the riverbank murder case, the scene of which was a block from the hotel.

After dinner, the team retired to the bar; Rankin sat in the cooling evening air on the veranda outside the bar analysing the day's events. He was certain that the murder of Theodorus was unrelated to the Mackay murder. A copycat murder – but why? He took the lift to his room, rang Wirth, had a short conversation with him, then rang Rhonda.

Next day, Rankin was at police headquarters early. He rang Bowman at home requesting notification of when the death certificate would be issued.

Backhouse and Johnson were informed of the will's terms – a surprise to them.

Rankin turned his attention to the riverside murder. The body had been discovered in a car parked at a riverbank carpark below the riverside road. The carpark serviced a commercial area. Full during the day, it is almost empty after six pm. It is not used at night, as there is plenty of parking in the city at night. Backhouse had stated the victim, a well-known local, had been garrotted. He was killed by a rope that had a noose at one end. The large knots stopped it from unwinding. The rope was left at the scene. The park was still taped off. During dinner the night before, the publican had told Rankin that the murdered man was often in the hotel private bar.

The victim was Terry Brighton, a former policeman, now a private investigator, process server, debt collector, and divorce investigator. Born at Rockhampton, he attended school locally, joined the force, and was transferred here after doing basic training at the academy in Brisbane. He spent his time here and in towns in the area. He played rugby league as a big loose-head forward for a local club and represented it in intercity matches. He also played against the Poms here. He resigned from the force when he was passed over for promotion.

He was a part of the local scene and generally well liked. His business operated from a small room at his home, with an answering service on his phone, and from the private bar of the hotel, which has a public phone. His diary was coded and his client was always Mr X. The person he was dealing with was always noted with initials if they were paying with cheque and Z if it was cash.

Some of his clients could be traced by the cheques paid into his bank, but he must have done a lot of work for cash, as there was a lot of money in his office safe.

There was solid payment in cash under z day before his death. His habits were drink, women, and punting.

Rankin thought of Button, the Brisbane sleazy divorce detective who could get in and out of any building and open most safes. Brighton could probably do the same. Rankin's mind was in overdrive. Brighton could have got the will information for someone, but who?

His team met at the police station, with Connors and Doyle absent. It was Blake's RDO; Connors and Doyle had been in the area of his house since 6am.

Addressing the remainder of the team at an early morning meeting, Rankin felt an air of anticipation. The phone records of all Theodorus sons-in-laws revealed all had called Viktor Comonio after his father's death, as Rankin expected. Rankin said, 'Brighton had been paid a large sum of cash money the day before he was garrotted. Backhouse and his team had decoded his diary and interviewed clients who could be traced by their cheque payments.

'They were mainly for domestic matters. They had secured his phone records, but a lot of calls were from public phones and untraceable, and many had not left messages on his answering service, just hung up. The big payment the day before his death was of real interest. We will never have the full picture because of cash work, the use of the hotel public phone, and his answering service. But it's a start.'

Rankin sat in the incident room after Backhouse and Johnson had left with his team. They were working on both cases.

Rankin studied the facts. Theodorus' married sons-in-law Calonsus and Sperous were big winners from his death. Their wives would hand their inheritance to their husbands, as was the Greek custom. They could now buy the business they managed. Condarus, Marree's ex-husband, was the big loser.

Rankin thought the two Rockhampton murders could be linked, but doubted it. Connors and Doyle remained on surveillance on Blake and Marree. 'We must find Mr X, but maybe he is a suspicious husband, who hired Brighton because he believed his wife was having an affair. A connection between Theodorus' murder and Brighton could exist. Brighton was murdered in a quiet riverside parking area used mainly by commercial business employees and owners. His murderer could have walked from the parking area, a block to the city main street. Someone could have noticed him, but we don't know what he or she looks like.'

Everyone had left the station. Rankin sat thinking – he needed to find something to break these murders open.

A police car arrived to take Rankin to the Rockhampton morgue for a meeting with the local forensic officer, Myers.

Myers said that in his experience, the method used to murder Brighton was odd. His neck was circled by a knotted rope with a loop at the end of it. The rope would have been placed over his head and pulled tight, the knots ensuring the rope did not slip back.

He was probably strangled by someone outside the vehicle, which had the driver's side window open.

The killer could have ensured the rope was secure behind one of the knots and left the victim to die. Brighton had been discovered by a person coming to collect his car at about 9pm after drinking at a hotel nearby after work. Myers believed Brighton had been dead about an hour when he examined the body at the murder scene. Rankin thanked Myers and left the morgue.

Back at the incident room Rankin thought the method of killing Brighton was definitely odd, but effective. A strong person had killed him.

The local detectives and Rankin's team were joined by Connors and Doyle at the station at 5pm. They all had a very busy day for no positive results, but Doyle and Connors had some very interesting news.

Connors and Doyle reported that Blake had left the house at 7am and driven off somewhere. Doyle followed him until he realised he was heading for the coast. He had come back and joined Connors. At 9am Marree had caught a bus to town and got off at her hangout, but had not gone in. 'She headed down the main street, quickly getting into a car. We followed it and got its number. When it pulled up at a house in the suburb of Allenstown, we drove on and came back in half an hour. The car was parked in an open garage, the house closed up. We rang in the car rego number; registered to Lance Lawrence Hillman. Further inquiries had revealed he worked for the same security firm as Blake. They were in the house for three hours, and then returned to the city.

'The driver dropped Marree at her pub and went back home. She had a few drinks and a meal at the New World Café restaurant and caught the five o'clock bus home.

'Christ,' said Black, 'This is a turn up for the books.' Rankin added it to the incident board.

Next morning both squads took on board the new information. Backhouse said, 'Very interesting, but how does it help us find the killers?'

Rankin told Connors and Doyle to put Hillman under surveillance starting tomorrow morning. Everyone else was to take the weekend off. They had done all they could. They had spent long hours, questioned hundreds and got statements for no real result. The firm told them that Hillman and Blake had RDO's for tomorrow, Saturday. Everyone left and Rankin was alone in the room. He again studied the incident board. He could not see a clear picture, but the answer was there somewhere. He rang Steele at Mackay, but he and his men were bogged down on the Cornelius Comonio murder.

The next day, Connors rang Rankin at midday telling him that Hillman was at the local race track and they were there and would stay with him. At 6pm, Doyle and Connors returned to their hotel and informed Rankin that Hillman had been joined by Blake and Marree, and the three had spent the afternoon together. Then all three had adjourned to the private bar at their hotel. Rankin told them to stay clear of the bar, as Blake or Hillman might realise they were police who had an interest in them. The two detectives moved to the private dining room, had supper, and joined Black and Kennedy at the pub opposite the police station.

On Sunday, Doyle and Connors were back on Hillman. Rankin went to his incident room at the police station. It was very quiet, as only a small staff was working. He focussed on the two incident boards trying to work out the solution to the murders of Theodorus and Brighton.

He still thought both murders had to be linked in some way. The relationship between Hillman and Marree was of interest as were Blake and Hillman. He contacted West, the security firm owner where Blake and Hillman worked, requesting details of all employees who were working the night of Theodorus murder. They could have seen something important and not realised it.

After a traditional Sunday lunch at the hotel, followed by a refreshing afternoon sleep, he reviewed the requested security firm rosters. At dinner that night, Connors and Doyle arrived and gave their report.

Hillman had picked up a young woman at a house in Wandal. They had gone to the beach for the day. It was a half hour drive. They followed his car, which he parked at the sea front. They changed to togs, covered themselves with sun screen oil, and had an hour's swim. They redressed in the change sheds, had an early lunch at the beach side café, then drove north to the rainforest area and went bush walking. 'We waited at their car as it was too exposed to follow them. We parked among other cars at the picnic area. They were gone three hours, and then drove back to Rockhampton and had dinner. Both entered the Wandal house and Hillman drove home later,' Connors said.

Rankin heard them out and said, 'Find out who the woman is – electoral roll duties for you Connors. Doyle will follow her if she leaves the house.' They all ate dinner, Rankin leaving as soon as he had finished his cup of tea. He drew up a chair in the cool outdoor area of the hotel and relaxed.

At ten, the next morning, Rankin, Kennedy, Black, Johnson, and Backhouse were in the incident room. Connors had been calling on houses in the street where Hillman's girlfriend lived. He took his badge stating he was an electoral officer, and a clip board and a pen and was pretending to check who lived at the houses to ensure they were on the roll. He started four houses before the girl's residence and continued four houses past.

Doyle went back to collect Connors and told him the girl had caught a bus to the city centre, entering a building which housed the legal firm, Bowman and Partners.

They joined the team at the police station and both delivered their report from yesterday and this morning to the assembled team. The woman's name was Elizabeth Margaret Gardener and she was now a person of interest. Connors had established that she was an articled clerk at Bowman's firm and her mother had proudly told Connors she was about to become engaged to a very nice young man. Connors assumed this was Hillman.

All detectives were brought up-to-date then departed to continue the investigation into Brighton and Theodorus murders. Black, Doyle, and Connors now joined them. They now had a connection with Bowman's legal firm – Hillman to Elizabeth Gardner and to Marree. Hillman was now a person of real interest.

From a telephone conversation with West, Rankin now knew that Hillman was ex-SAS, capable, sober, and reliable. Rankin told West not to bother Hillman about his call, and they would see Hillman if necessary. He now knew Hillman was capable of killing Theodorus and Brighton, but why?

Rankin studied Hillman's schedule the night of Theodorus murder.

He analysed the players involved. Blake ex-military, Hillman ex-SAS, both now security guards, Brighton ex-police then private investigator, debt collector and process server. Marree, disowned daughter, living with an older man and having a lover, Hillman, who had young girl friend who was an articled clerk employed by Bowman and Partners. Theodorus' murder made Marree a rich woman.

Somehow it all centred around Marree and her inheritance. But who knew about it? Hillman was high on his list. He had a link to Bowman's office where the will was kept and was Marree's lover. Rankin studied Hillman's security route the night of the murder of Theodorus and compared it with the last time he was on this run.

He felt a pulse go through him as he saw the card time registered between two places he serviced. Rankin drove to a car service building where Hillman had checked in at ten fifty-five and then drove to his next client. It was a four minute drive, but his check in at his next client was recorded as fourteen minutes later on the night of the murder and that time gap corresponded with the time of the murder. Rankin went back to the service building.

A number of cars and a few motorcycles were inside the fenced off area beside it. He knew they were finished jobs waiting to be picked up. Rankin drove from there to the unit where Theodorus was murdered. Even in the daytime traffic, it only took five minutes. Rankin now believed he knew how Hillman had killed the old Greek.

He would have had keys to the service centre yard and could have taken one of the serviced vehicles left overnight. His embossed security car would have been left in the yard and picked up after he killed the old Greek. He then checked in at the next place on his list. Rankin decided to have all vehicles left overnight dusted for prints. He was at the police station at midday. Hillman was on night shift and would probably be at home. Rankin contacted Kennedy and Black and instructed them to bring in Hillman.

Half an hour later, a very angry Hillman was in the interview room with Rankin, Kennedy, and Backhouse. The rules of interview had been explained to Backhouse, who Rankin included for local politics – say nothing unless asked. Rankin started the tape recorder stating the reason for the inquiry, those present, time, and date.

Rankin said to Hillman, 'We have reason to believe you could help with the investigation into the death of Arron Theodorus.'

Hillman sat back and his muscles bulked under his T-shirt. He was average build, but appeared very fit. He had short hair and angry hazel eyes. He said nothing.

Showing Hillman a copy of his work schedule for the night in question, Rankin continued, 'On the night of the murder, your key-ins show a fifteen minute break at the time of the murder, can you account for this?'

Hillman started to laugh. Kennedy said, 'Murder is not funny.'

Hillman said, 'Definitely not, but you clowns are.'

Backhouse rose to move towards Hillman, but Rankin, in a firm voice, said, 'Sit down.'

Backhouse glared at Hillman. 'We don't have to take this from him, Sir!'

Sneering, Hillman said, 'Any time you fancy yourself, one on one, not two holding me while you belt me in the cells. Behind any pub or where you want it.'

Kennedy said, 'You're threatening a police officer!'

Now laughing Hillman said, 'No, giving him options.'

Rankin banged the table and said, 'Enough of this macho talk. Let's get on with this enquiry. Tell me the reason for your laughter and sarcasm?'

Hillman said, 'I have nothing to say except to the papers and TV stations about your shoddy investigation. You are so desperate to close the case that you tried to fit me up, but a solicitor will expose this.'

Rankin noted the time and turned the recorder off. They left Hillman in the room and went outside.

Rankin sent for Connors and Doyle. They entered the room with Rankin and Backhouse. Hillman said, 'The second division. I hope they are brighter than the first.'

Rankin said, 'You want to play hard-ball – the game has started. Detective Sergeants Doyle and Connors have some information you might want to hear.'

Hillman looked bored and Doyle said, 'On the third of this month a woman, Marree, was observed leaving the house where she lives with a Simon Blake and catching a bus to the city. There she entered a car and was driven to an address in the suburbs of Allenstown. The car was registered to an L. L. Hillman who was found to live there.'

Hillman was quiet now as he digested Connor's statement. 'Further, Hillman went to the beach last Sunday with a Miss Elizabeth Gardener whose mother stated she was soon to be engaged. Elizabeth works at a law firm in the city. On the Saturday before you, Marree, and her de facto husband were at the local races. I do not believe Blake knows you are having an affair with his woman and your intended also doesn't know about it. Things can change.'

Hillman was very still and said, 'Touché! Chief inspector, what do you want to know?'

Rankin said, 'Your movements at the time of the Theodorus murder.'

Hillman said, 'I logged in at a car garage at around ten fifty-five, drove to the old people's home nearby, had a smoke talked to the girls coming off shift, went to our next client logged in and rang in.'

Rankin demanded names of the women he saw at the old person's home.

'Glenda Markwell, Elizabeth Bray, and a woman who was with them. She was picked up by a man, probably her husband.'

'Where do Glenda and Elizabeth live?'

Hillman said, 'Northside, I believe. They would be on the phone as both are care nurses.'

The detective left the room. A few phone calls verified Hillman's statement. The night matron had seen Hillman parked near their office and knew the time, as did Glenda and the third woman. When they located the woman, she said she had looked her watch when talking to Hillman as her husband was running late. It was a minute after eleven.

Rankin, Connors, and Doyle went back to the interview room.

Hillman said, 'My private life should be of no concern to you.'

Rankin said, 'Provided it is not linked to the Brighton and Theodorus murders, it doesn't. Your intended works for a law firm in the city. Did you ever ask her for information about firm business?'

'Many times, discretely,' said Hillman, 'I wanted the information for the firm I work for. There is a good bonus for bringing new work and where she works needs some security, it's so old fashioned and backward. You could open the place with a tin opener.'

'It has a secure safe,' said Kennedy.

'A key type with the keys kept in fragile office drawers… sure, Fort Knox.'

Connors said, 'She has told you a lot about her firm?'

Hillman said, 'Yes, but did not know she was doing it – just idle talk on many occasions.'

Rankin said, 'Marree could have money coming from her father's estate.'

Hillman said, 'A bear might fly. If she did, she would be an attractive proposition, but not to me on a permanent basis.'

Rankin turned off the tape after giving the time and date. He said, 'We will keep in touch, but you are free to go.'

Hillman said, 'What about…'

Rankin said, 'We are not the keeper of morals. Unless you have kept something from us, your secrets are safe. Is there anything more?'

Hillman shook his head and they all left the room.

Backhouse asked, 'What happened, Sir?'

Rankin answered, 'He is clean, perfect alibi, that's why he was so smug.'

Rankin was deflated. He had been so wrong. He had reached the end of the line with this case, and the Mackay murder of Comonio was still unsolved.

But that murder was different. There was no financial benefit to anyone from the Mackay murder.

Police had been tied up a week on the Theodorus and Brighton murders. Hundreds of statements had been made to CIB and uniformed police. They were being taken off the case with a back-log of work to do. Johnson and Backhouse had been fulltime on the Brighton murder – a mystery inside a mystery.

Rankin sent Kennedy, Connors and Black back to Brisbane. Doyle remained in Rockhampton. Rankin gave Doyle a lot of work as he was on a learning curve.

Bowman advised him the Theodorus death certificate was to hand and beneficiaries of his estate would be notified that day, Friday.

Marree would be a big winner and now a rich woman. He wondered briefly the fate of her present relationship with Blake and possibly Hillman. Money can alter plans.

He knew Doyle, Backhouse, and Johnson would be at the private bar in the hotel opposite police headquarters. Probably discussing his major blunder over Hillman. He had never suffered with depression, but he was not a happy man when he had phoned his report to Commissioner Wirth. He would now phone an unhappy wife. He had missed another school function that was important to her and his children. He went to bed and slept deeply from mental fatigue.

Next morning, looking at the overflowing incident board, looking for new combinations, Rankin did not notice Doyle walking in the door.

Doyle said, 'Four winners from Theodorus murder and all have alibis. The husbands of the daughters will control the money they inherited. The loser is Marree's ex-husband who manages the big New World café restaurant. He could be out of a job.'

Rankin thought over his words. Marree's husband, Condarus, was a two-time loser from the Theodorus murder. A middle-aged city businessman running Theodorus biggest café, he had custody of his and Marree's two children and employed a full-time live-in housekeeper.

Besides losing her inheritance, his job was now in jeopardy. The trustees could sell the business or the other brothers-in-laws could buy it and run it without him.

Managing the city's top café restaurant gave him social position in the non-Greek local community and a large income. Unlike the other Greeks who worked for wages, he had a profit sharing arrangement with Theodorus. He was a nothing without his current job.

Rankin went through all of the winners. They were advantaged by his death and had to be suspect. The sons-in-law could have hired someone to kill Theodorus. They were the big winners, as was Marree. Despite the local opinion, Blake could have murdered Theodorus. Rankin believed Marree would waste her legacy and leave her children very little.

Then another option entered Rankin's mind and he now thought he had the answer to both murders. It was out of centre and a big assumption.

Doyle and Rankin went to Blake's home; no one was home. Doyle had a hunch Marree and Simon Blake would be would be celebrating somewhere, but Rankin had other ideas.

He thought she would be looking for a new car today and looking at a new house Monday, if she wanted to stay in this city. They found Blake and Marree at the Mercedes Benz dealer admiring a few new models, a smooth looking salesman hovering nearby.

Trying to catch the salesman's eye, the detectives were swiftly fobbed off. 'I am busy at the moment, please wait in the office.'

Rankin showed his badge, sent the salesman back to the office, and said to Marree, 'Mr Blake knows me, you must be happy, Marree, now a wealthy woman.'

Marree smiled. 'And Simon too. He wants to keep working so we are going to buy the firm he works for. He can be an office manager and Lance Hillman, his second-in-command will eventually be the firm's manager when he marries the girl he goes with and settles down. Then Daddy and I are going for an overseas holiday. *Daddy* thought Rankin, *A term endearment. Marree is a child at heart.*

'We are going out tonight, as he has the day off. He will be working tomorrow night, as Mr West needs him.' She was still gazing lovingly at the new luxury car – never took her eye off it, mesmerized.

Rankin wished them the best as he and Doyle left. The salesman hastened to join Marree.

In the car, Rankin said, 'She is in mortal danger, Doyle, and is innocent of the fact. Let's find Lance Hillman.'

Doyle was confused, but said nothing. Rankin had rung West, the security firm's owner, and established that Hillman was on the midnight shift last night and had been given Sunday off, but would be working Monday. They drove past Hillman's house and his car was in the carport. Surveillance had established he slept until around two pm when he was on night shift, drifting to the pub down the road about three pm. He drank sparingly and played pool, meeting his intended sometimes after she finished work.

Rankin and Doyle returned to police headquarters to prepare the next move. At three pm, Rankin and Doyle were at Hillman's house. He appeared surprised to see them. And more so, when Rankin told him and Doyle his plan, and the job they had to do. Hillman could decline it, but Doyle could not.

Hillman said, 'Why not use local police?'

Rankin stated, 'A shotgun could be involved and the murderer has to be caught in the act. It is a job for someone trained like you. Our police here would be a danger to themselves.'

Hillman agreed to help. He said. 'I have great affection for Marree and will assist you, but who are we dealing with?'

Rankin said, 'I'm not sure. I have been wrong in the past, as you know.'

Hillman said, 'Count me in. Life has become boring and when I'm married it will be mundane.'

The afternoon passed peacefully. Rankin was considering his next play. He was worried about the risks, but confident of Doyle and Hillman. Tomorrow's planned action was the last throw of the dice for the investigation of the Theodorus and Brighton murders. He thought he knew who the killer was, and the motive, but then he had been so wrong about Hillman. He was going out on a limb using a private security officer on a policeman's job. His operation was full of traps and only he, Doyle and Hillman knew about it. Doyle would not have a drink tomorrow until it was over.

Sunday, he and Doyle went to the coast for the day. That afternoon Rankin was at the pub across the road from Blake about six pm as drinkers were leaving the pub by the side door. He showed his badge to the publican who was apprehensive. Rankin told him he had no interest in illegal hotel trading. He told him what he wanted. At 7pm, Rankin, Doyle, and Hillman were in the unlit front porch of the hotel. Blake left the house at 8pm to go to work. When he was gone, Doyle and Hillman went into the house's yard, silently taking up positions in the front and back of the house. Rankin stayed at the hotel patio with a clear view of the house and its yard.

An hour later, the house in darkness, a small Vespa motorcycle came past the hotel and parked in a parking bay on the other side of the street. A man dismounted, looked around the deserted street, drew something from the pouch at the back of the seat, and entered Blake's yard.

Doyle moved silently from his post in the shadows at the front of the house, following him. Hillman watched as the man pulled something from his right hand and knocked on the back door of the back porch. The kitchen light went on. The intruder wrapped the rope he was holding tightly around both hands. Marree was saying, 'Who are you? What do you want?'

Getting no answer, she turned the porch light on and angrily flung the door open. The intruder put the rope over her head as Hillman crashed tackled him, both landing heavily on the wooden porch. Doyle cuffed the struggling intruder.

Rankin raced across the road to the house. Marree was standing in a daze as the porch light threw light on the three men struggling on the porch.

Marree stared in disbelief at the intruder gasping, 'Gorgio!' Confusion clouding her face, she said, 'Gorgio, why do you want to kill me?'

Gorgio snarled, 'You robbed me of my inheritance, you slut. You embarrassed me by divorcing me. You are a low-life moll and a disgrace to the Greek nation. You are better off dead.'

Rankin took the rope from around Marree neck, bagged it and the driving gloves Condarus was wearing. Condarus was led away by Doyle with Hillman close by. Using Marree's phone, Rankin telephoned for a police car and van, and then phoned West to have Blake relieved and sent home.

Rankin stayed with the sobbing Marree until the police car arrived to remove Condarus to the police station. The Vespa was loaded onto a police vehicle.

Blake was soon on the scene. He was met at the door by a sobbing Marree. 'Gorgio was going to kill me, Daddy.'

Blake cuddled her. 'It's all right baby, Daddy's home and you're safe.' She clung to him like a child. Blake said, 'What the hell's going on, Mr Rankin?'

Rankin told him. Blake exploded. 'You used Marree as bait!'

Without missing a beat, Rankin said, 'She was always safe.'

Blake said, 'Why did her ex-husband want to kill her?'

Marree sobbed, 'He was angry my father left me money, which he thinks should have been his.'

Rankin said nothing and walked to a waiting police car.

The knotted rope seized from Condarus was identical to the one that had killed Brighton.

At the police station, Condarus was being held in cell. The duty officer met Rankin as he entered headquarters, 'He demanded a solicitor.'

Rankin said, 'He can get one tomorrow morning. Doyle get the police photographer here as soon as possible. I want a clear photo of Condarus and fifty copies made.' Rankin rang Meyers, the local forensic officer, who was home, and told him to be at the station at 7am tomorrow.

Condarus was brought from his cell to an interview room. Rankin and Doyle sat opposite him at a table. He said, 'I demand a solicitor.'

Doyle said, 'You have not been charged with anything. We merely want have a chat.'

Condarus said, 'I have nothing to say.'

Rankin said, 'But I have. You attempted to murder your ex-wife tonight.'

'Not true. I went there to talk to her about supporting our children.'

'You went to the back of the house to see her?'

'I didn't want to be seen knocking on her front door when her de facto was not home.'

Pointing to the evidence bag Rankin said, 'You had this rope in your hands, were wearing gloves, and threw it over your estranged wife's head.' He produced the knotted rope from the evidence bag.

Condarus said, 'I merely wanted to frighten her and get her to pay for some of the children's upkeep.'

'My men removed it from your ex-wife's neck.'

'I only wanted to frighten her. You are trying to frame me and I want a solicitor.'

Rankin said, 'You said to her a number of threatening things.'

'In anger, but not meant.'

'You were wearing gloves when you arrived on the Vespa,' Rankin said.

'I always wear them when I ride my Vespa and when driving my car. I demand a solicitor.'

'You have not been charged with anything,' Doyle repeated, 'When you are charged a solicitor will be here to represent you.'

Condarus stood. 'I refuse to answer any more questions.' He was taken back to his cell.

Rankin said, 'Enough for tonight, let him stew.'

Next morning, Rankin and Doyle were at the station early, Myers had collected the gloves and rope. The police photographer arrived and took photos of Condarus and left.

Backhouse and Johnson arrived at the station, angry that they had been left out of last night's operation and more so because Rankin had used a civilian.

Rankin told them to get all available information on Condarus. 'I want private and business phone records for him and Brighton, his banking records, private and business – bank statements and cheque book butts.'

The 50 photos of Condarus arrived while he was speaking. Rankin handed them out. 'Now you have a photo to work with, go over all the original investigation again with all police available. They left with photo of Condarus. The photos made a difference.

Police now knew what they were looking for. A link between Condarus and Brighton had been established because the rope used was identical to the one that had killed Brighton.

Rankin now had a theory of why Condarus was involved in both murders. Rankin said to Doyle, 'Moment of truth soon. I believe we are dealing with a very evil and cunning person.'

At nine o'clock, Condarus was given a phone and rang a solicitor. The solicitor, Day, arrived at the station in thirty minutes, interviewing Condarus in an interview room with two constables at the door. At 10am, Day notified Rankin that he was ready to proceed. But Rankin was not.

Myers rang him at five past ten and gave him a short report, which sent a pulse through him. He said an assistant would deliver his report to him in ten minutes.

Meanwhile, Blake, and Marree arrived at police headquarters. A much calmer woman gave a statement, which a police stenographer typed. Marree checked the statement and signed it. Blake said, 'Condarus could have been armed. '

Rankin replied, 'We were ready if he was, but a gun going off makes a lot of noise late at night in a quiet suburb. The rope was a silent killer.' Casually, Rankin asked Marree if she had a will and she said no.

Condarus and Day were waiting in the interview room. Rankin ignored Day's complaint of the long wait he and his client had to endure. The tape recorder was set up giving the time, date and reason for the interview and who was present, including Doyle and a detective constable. Backhouse and Johnson were investigating Condarus' affairs. The rules of questioning were explained. Rankin said, 'Mr Condarus, are these your gloves?' He stated for the tape recording that he was showing Condarus a pair of light gloves.

Sulkily, the reply came, 'So what, I explained their purpose to you last night.'

Rankin said, 'I am now showing Mr Condarus two, three foot lengths of knotted rope. Have you seen these before Mr Condarus?'

'Only the one I made up. As I told you before, I am being set up by you police.'

Rankin said, 'You threw one of these ropes around your ex-wife neck attempting to kill her.'

Condarus said, 'I wanted to frighten her into contributing to the upkeep of our children.'

Rankin closed the interview.

Rankin and Doyle went to the suspect's home and showed their badges to his housekeeper. They entered his office and saw the big chiming clock which gave Condarus an alibi for when Theodorus killed. At the back of the house was an iron shed with a workbench inside it. There were irrigation pipes to be attached to lawn sprinklers cut to size.

There was a vice and a coil of rope. They left the yard and noticed small trees tied with rope to straighten them.

The same rope size as in the shed and the rope that killed Brighton, but it was a very common item.

Back at the police station, Rankin rang Commissioner Wirth requesting the State Forensic Officer Mullins be in Rockhampton as soon as possible.

'Now the real work starts. We must establish motive and opportunity to murder both Theodorus and Brighton.'

Doyle said, 'I understand that anger over something was the reason he wanted to murder Marree. But his statement at the murder scene that she had robbed him of his inheritance I don't understand.'

Rankin said, 'Marree's sisters, as is the custom, will turn their inherence over to their husbands, but not Marree. Condarus gets nothing. I believe Condarus hired Brighton to get the information about the Theodorus will. Arron Theodorus was getting old and Gorgio believed that he would be rewarded for rearing the children, and for the embarrassment Marree had caused him. He hired Brighton to find out the contents or the will, and as Hillman said, the office and drawers with the safe key in them could be opened with a tin opener.'

Doyle said, 'So Brighton got details of the terms of the will. The will contents angered Condarus so much that he planned the murder of Theodorus. But first, he had to kill Brighton to close the circle. He then attempted to kill Marree over her inheritance, which he believed should be his.'

Rankin said, 'Local police have been flat out on the two murder investigations and I believe we can bring them together. I believe Theodorus was an X in his book – one of Brighton's investigations.'

Johnson and Backhouse were back at the station examining the private and business phone accounts of Condarus. If he was a cash payer, payments to Brighton would not be recorded in his bank statements, but in his personal diary. Rankin told them to check Condarus' personal bank statements against the large amounts payed to Brighton in cash the day Brighton was murdered. Rankin believed the money was taken from the café till and a private cheque written to replace it, to balance the books.

Both squads working at the police station were very interested in the course both investigations had taken. Rankin was relaxed. He had all the aces and believed Mullins would give him the joker. All detectives were working at the office. Backhouse and Johnson had amassed a heap of phone accounts and bank statements and were linking them together.

Condarus had a different solicitor now – an older and more confident man. He was Bowman's senior criminal solicitor, Rochdale. He asked to see Rankin privately. They went to an interview room and Rochdale got straight to business. His client would admit to trying to terrorise his ex-wife, in the hope of forcing her to support her children, but he was adamant that he did not intend to kill her. He said Rankin would be hard put to prove otherwise. 'His verbal outburst was made under strain, and in the circumstances was understandable. He knew the other husbands benefited from Theodorus death, but he had no benefit as he and Marree were no longer married.'

Rankin rejected his offer. Rochdale then went back to Condarus' cell, remaining there with his client.

179

Rankin brought Condarus to the interview room with his solicitor. Rankin, Doyle, and Backhouse were present as he turned on the recorder and gave the usual details. Rankin charged Condarus with the attempted murder of his ex-wife. This did not surprise Rochdale. 'My client had nothing to say.'

Condarus was taken back to his cell. A brief conference took place between solicitor and client. Rochdale hurried back to his office.

The local detectives thought Rankin's swift laying of the charge of attempted murder of Marree was provable. Rankin was now confident he had the solutions to both murders. He picked Mullins up at the airport and told him what he wanted. Mullins joined Myers at the forensic laboratory. In an hour, Mullins had the answer. Rankin summoned Rochdale back to the station and in his presence and with Backhouse and Johnson, charged Condarus with Theodorus' murder. There was a stunned silence. Rankin left the interview room and Condarus was escorted back to the cells. Rochdale followed his client.

Back in the squad room, Rankin was busily preparing a fresh white board. He had everyone's attention.

Condarus: motive for murder of Theodorus – money. Motive for attempted murder of Marree – money. Doyle and the local detectives looked on. Motive for murder of Brighton – the man knew too much.

He told the gathered detectives, 'Condarus had engaged him to find the contents of the will, as Theodorus was getting older and he wanted to know if his effort in raising Theodorus grandchildren would be recognised. He was angry when he learnt it was not.

180

'When Condarus decided to kill Theodorus, he could not risk Brighton putting it together. Blake was accidently, almost framed for the murder.

'Condarus knew he would be the last person that the investigation would consider for the murder. He had lost everything when Theodorus was murdered. But he had to move fast to ensure his inheritance after Marree got her money. He knew she would splurge it on a car then a home in the best suburb. The property would be owned as joint tenants with Blake. He would then own it on her death. She would be spending money that he considered his, so he would have to kill her as soon as possible. Theodorus was not murdered in anger but in cold blood in the overall plans of Condarus to secure what he considered was his rightful money.

'We would have been at a loss with two strangling rope deaths. We would have been trying to establish a connection between Marree and Brighton and who hated them. Marree estate would have passed to her children unnoticed, but we foiled his plans to riches.'

Johnson, Doyle, and Backhouse were staring at him, their faces showing the confusion they were feeling. Doyle asked, 'How does he benefit?'

Rankin said, 'Who benefited if Marree was killed?' Rankin waited for an answer, eventually Backhouse said, 'Her children.' Rankin continued, 'Who would be in charge of the money?'

'Condarus as their guardian,' said Doyle.

The three detectives then saw what a diabolical person Condarus was. A devious plan, which almost succeeded.

'Mullins and Myers found iron filings in a workshop Condarus had at his home, which match the steel in the cut down shotgun that was used to kill his father-in-law. Mullins stated there was a coil of rope in the Condarus workshop and its cutting pattern by a pair of hedge clippers in his shed matched the ends of the ropes Condarus had used. Any questions?'

There was silence as the detectives considered what had happened. Rankin said, 'We have a strong case. Johnson and Backhouse will continue the investigation of the Brighton murder. We have enough to send him down for Theodorus' murder. Brighton was murdered by him, but our case against him rests on motive and the rope that Condarus had. Mullins evidence of the filings matching the gun barrels and that a pair of hedge clippers he owns match the way the rope ends that murdered Brighton were cut. His clock alibi could have been arranged by turning back the clock to make it chime.

'All of this enhances our case against Condarus, but is insufficient to charge him with Brighton's murder at this time. But local police can handle that. The sooner the better, so that we can charge him. Put more pressure on him, sulky, whingeing bugger, he will fold like a sack of potatoes once he hears the evidence. He is neither smart nor mentally strong.'

A few days later, Rankin, Doyle, Myers, and Mullins gave evidence in the Magistrates Court. The Magistrate, satisfied with police evidence, ordered that Condarus remain in jail to be tried at the next sittings of the Supreme Court. He was facing charges for murder and attempted murder.

Rankin thanked the detectives and the superintendent for the uniform police he made available in the case. Rankin and Doyle flew home. Backhouse and Johnson had already commenced the final inquiries which would result in a third murder charge. Rankin thought it odd that so many mourned Brighton.

The thirty pieces of silver were a red herring. But then Condarus was not real smart in the end.

Commissioner Wirth was happy with the squad's work. The Rockhampton superintendent was happy with the result. But Steele was still floundering with the Mackay Greek Murder.

Rankin sat back on the plane to Brisbane and relaxed. It would be good to get home. This case had drained him mentally and physically. He decided to take his wife and sons to Noosa for the next weekend and get back on side with his wife.

CHAPTER 8

WINTON UPDATE

Commissioner Wirth had forwarded a request to his New South Wales counterpart to consider investigating the information gathered by Rankin's homicide squad while investigating the murder at Winton in north Queensland. The Coroner had found the death of the grazier, his wife, and her son was murder–suicide, but Rankin was not convinced he was right.

Briscoe, a detective sergeant at Parramatta, had received the Queensland file for assessment.

After conducting interviews with Dane Clifford, Clive Roberts and their six mates, Briscoe concluded that all men had alibis for the likely dates of the Winton Murders. Ditto their wives. Five of their mates were married with children. The sixth man was divorced, but had custody of two children. All the men formed the front pack of the local rugby union club and all expressed a hatred of the murdered youth, Steven. They considered him a sex fiddler with their children.

The ex-wife of the divorced man, born of Syrian parents, had married a grazier who lived in the Middleton district in north-west Queensland, about thirty miles south of Winton. Police investigated the woman prior to her first marriage. She had been divorced after four years of marriage and had two children. They were now in the ex-husband's custody, but she has phone contact with them.

184

Now that her ex has another woman, the anger over her leaving has gone out of him. He keeps her up to date with the children's progress, but refuses to allow physical contact despite her visiting rights. In a report to Wirth, Briscoe enclosed her phone number and a short report on her. She is an ex-police officer. Police records show she was a good officer but with a short fuse. She retired from the service after a serious car accident, which caused both hands to be mangled. The ugly damage was now covered by light, gloves.

Six months after her divorce, she remarried and left the force. She now has two children from her second marriage. Commissioner Wirth did not think the New South Wales Police report took things much further. However, he left the report on Rankin's desk with a note for Rankin to phone Briscoe if any queries came to mind.

Rankin found the report interesting. *An interesting woman, the Syrian, another Sydney connection,* he thought. He phoned Morris and requested a discrete background report on her lifestyle in Winton. *After an active working and matrimonial life in Sydney, Winton must sometimes be a challenge.* Morris was informed she was a former police officer.

CHAPTER 9

WINTON REVISTED

On the Monday after the Noosa weekend break, Rankin was back at his office early, anticipating the report from Morris. It arrived mid-morning.

The Syrian woman, now Mrs Goodwin, had been in Winton the Friday of the Harvey killings.

She always collected her children at Winton on Friday unless they had a special weekend trip on. The children boarded with her husband's sister in Winton during the week, as her husband's property was over a hundred miles from Winton.

That weekend, they were going to Longreach for a school get together and would be billeted out. Mrs Goodwin had not travelled to Longreach for the weekend. She had brought a property vehicle to be serviced at the dealers and collected the vehicle at 12pm. The vehicle had been booked in for service a month before. She loaded groceries from her rural agent, had lunch at the Greek café and farewelled her children. *Nothing out of the ordinary there,* Rankin thought.

The plane that brought Steven to Winton had landed at one pm. It was assumed by Morris that Mrs Goodwin went back home after farewelling her children. Morris had not questioned her as he was instructed only to gather information on her.

She was a member of the local rifle club and worked on the property with her husband.

She helped with the removal of dingoes, wild pigs, and kangaroos. She was said to be a deadly shot. She did not serve on any school committee or attend CWA events.

Rankin realised it was probably only a coincidence that she was in Winton the day that the young paedophile had landed there. A discrete call to the phone exchange disclosed from its records that a Sydney call from her ex-husband had been made to her two nights before. Further, she had called the Harveys on the night of the killings and again in the following week. But everyone at the Tedsley Downs homestead was dead by then.

Too much of a coincidence, Rankin thought. He pondered the information and made a decision. For the first time, Rankin started to put things together. Sufficiently confident of Wirth's measured support, Rankin organised flights to Winton for Doyle and himself for Friday.

Doyle, the newest recruit was inexperienced but a quick learner and very observant.

Rankin and Doyle flew to Winton and Morris met them at the airport at 1pm. They went to police headquarters. Rankin paid his respects to the senior sergeant before the three detectives had lunch at the Greek café. They were waiting for Mrs Goodwin to collect her children and take them home for the weekend. She arrived in town, went to their rural agent, and collected some merchandise.

Swiftly but discretely, Rankin moved beside her, showing his badge, saying he wanted to talk to her about her movements the day of the Harvey killings. For the first time, Rankin took in her appearance. She was dark-skinned, with alert brown eyes and wore gloves that stood out in the local heat. Businesslike, Mrs Goodwin said she had to pick up her children. She would take them to her husband's sister who lived nearby, and then she would be free to be interviewed. A meeting was arranged to take place at the Greek café. Half an hour later, she strode into the café.

The four of them sat at a table at the back of the dining area. Rankin said, 'We want to talk to you about the Harvey killings.'

She shrugged and said, 'What do you want to know?'

Doyle, leading off, replied, 'Your movements that day?'

'I had the vehicle serviced, said good bye to my kids, who were going away for the weekend, had a quick meal here, then an hour's drive towards Kynuna. I was feeling isolated without my kids. I saw Gwen Harvey in the main street with a teenage boy who I believed was a paedophile who was going to live in the district. I drove back to Winton and then home to the station.'

Rankin followed up. 'You have not protested about what we are doing?'

With a wry expression, she replied, 'I have been under observation for weeks and wondered when I would be approached. I was a cop and always read numberplates and associate them with people. The police here have a lot to learn about surveillance. They are complete amateurs and cretins and should be sent to a police school to learn how to do it.'

Morris' face went red, but he said nothing.

Doyle took up the questioning. 'You were a police officer in Sydney?'

Mrs Goodwin responded, 'As you are so interested in me, I will give you my life story. I was born and bred in the government housing towers at the bottom of Kings Cross, joined the police force at age eighteen, and worked the Cross and Darlinghurst for years – under cover in the drug squad and in the vice squad until a bad car accident wrecked my hands. I was no longer suitable for any police undercover work as my hands are now encased in gloves and that is noticeable. I retired to office work as I could still type, but I resigned from boredom and joined a private security firm.

'I met a fellow while working at a football final and married him, but it did not work out. He got custody of our young children. Working at a national horse sale at Dubbo, I met my present husband and we now have two children. I'm now a grazier's wife, but I find the women boring. Their conversations are mainly about rain, the local show, race meetings, and what to wear to them. But I am happy enough. Gwen Harvey was a breath of fresh air when we often met, as she was worldly. Her husband was the silent type.'

No real surprises there, thought Rankin. 'When was the last time you saw Gwen Harvey?'

Mrs Goodwin replied, 'The Friday she is believed to have been murdered. She had her son with her. I didn't seek her out. This was not something to be sorted out in public. My ex-husband rang me and said our children had been sexually assaulted, as had had many of his mate's children.

189

'The perpetrator was Gwen Harvey's son, Steven. And now she was bringing him to Winton. My ex-husband said that no police action had been taken, as it could not be proven. Children's evidence was insufficient. But Gwen Harvey was taking him out of Sydney.'

Rankin said, 'This angered you?'

Mrs Goodwin looked at Rankin as if he were a backward child. 'That's a bit of an understatement. Do you think we wanted him here? I typed up letters to all schools in the area, PC associations, children's clubs, and the local paper warning them of the paedophile's presence in the area. I enveloped and stamped them and was going to send them after I had talked to Gwen Harvey. I wanted to explain to Gwen what I was going to do as I liked her and thought she should know what I was doing.

'I rang her after I got home, about six pm, but her phone didn't answer. I rang her twice the next day, and again got no answer. I thought she and Harvey were away somewhere and her son was with the workers. I was not releasing the letters until I told her. Twelve days after I saw her, what had happened at Tedsley was public knowledge. I have things to do and must leave you soon. The letters are in the glove box of my vehicle send one of your men to get them.'

Rankin did and opened one and read its contents. He handed the letter back to her.

Tucking the letter into her handbag, she stood, smiled, and said, 'Must be off.'

Rankin said, 'We have not finished here yet.'

Gathering her shoulder bag, Mrs Goodwin said, 'But I have, Chief Inspector. The coroner has given his verdict. Stop fishing in dry creek beds.' Mrs Goodwin strode out of the café towards her ute.

'Arrogant Arab bitch,' said Morris. Doyle laughed and said, 'She was deliberately baiting you, and laughing at us all. She has covered all bases either by fact or design.'

Requesting another pot of tea from a passing waitress, Rankin collected his thoughts. Everyone, including the Coroner, considered the deaths were murder-suicide; however, it did not sit well with Rankin. Mrs Goodwin was the last throw of the dice.

Mrs Goodwin, a trained police woman, would know how to handle a gun and cover her tracks, she had motive and time to murder Harvey, his wife and her son.

Back at the station, Rankin wrote on the white board.

Suspect: Mrs X

Motive: Revenge for what happed to her children in Sydney

Opportunity: Yes, after establishing Gwen Harvey was in town, she could have driven to the Tedsley Downs and been there long before Gwen Harvey and Steven arrived. Motive, but no eye witness.

Morris said, 'But why kill Harvey, killing Steven, the young paedophile, was understandable, and maybe Gwen Harvey, but not her husband. If we can establish she was on the Tedsley Downs road, we can negate her statement that says she drove towards Kynuna.'

'Morris interviewed everyone he found who had been on the Tedsley Downs road the day of the killings. But someone could have noticed her and thought nothing of it at the time. The killings were accepted as murder-suicide long before the coroner brought in his verdict.'

Doyle asked, 'What is your theory, Chief?'

Going over old material Rankin replied, 'Wine as the final drink for Harvey at the kitchen table when rum was available at his office was odd, as was the pressure lamp beside the table and leaving the fly screen door open. But a woman visitor who knew his wife would oblige Harvey to be hospitable and offer her hospitality. A glass of wine, perhaps. From the amount of wine used from the bottle, he could have poured two glasses and then a second two. Something Harvey said or did could have upset his visitor, who I believe had only called to talk to him about the paedophile he would be harbouring under his roof. She intended to then wait for Gwen Harvey and have it out with her.

'She could have been at Tedsley before Gwen Harvey. In anger, his visitor shot him with his own gun because of something he said or did or she is evil beyond comprehension and killed Harvey to close the circle.' Remember, New South Wales police said Mrs Goodwin had a short fuse. The die was cast, she would have to kill Gwen and her son or answer for killing Harvey. After killing Harvey, she poured her untouched wine back into the bottle, washed and dried her glass and put it back in the glass shelf. She would have been gloved as always. She then met Mrs Harvey and her son in the yard between the open garage and the homestead.

192

'She killed them and set the scene for Harvey's apparent suicide. The screen door being left ajar when she left was probably of little interest to her and not noticed.'

Morris was sceptical, but thought it feasible. It all would depend on the reinterviewing of land owners along the Tedsley Downs Road. 'Together with other officers, I will intently question everyone along the Tedsley Downs road again, get a photograph of her car model from the dealer, and have it publisher with an appeal for help. That model is a dime a dozen here, but being driven by a woman, it could have been noticed.'

Rankin said, 'Even if you prove she was in the vicinity of the murders she could claim that she was driving to the property, changed her mind, and passed Gwen on the way back, but had not stopped. She will admit the Kynuna drive was incorrect, but say she didn't want to be known to be in the area of the murder. She is ex-police and understands evidence. Her story, backed by the letters and phone calls, is at present an iron clad alibi. Unless you find an eye witness who saw her going or coming through the station grid, we have nothing. She is an ex-police woman and knows this.'

Rankin and Doyle were driven to the airport next morning and flew home. The trail was cold in the Winton killings. Rankin realised it was no closer to being solved. Mrs Goodwin was firmly in his frame, but proof was needed and there was none.

Morris was noted in Rankin's black book as a future recruit to the State Homicide Squad. The summer had set in and the November heat had all office windows closed. Things were quiet and his men were not busy.

CHAPTER 10

CAIRNS' MURDERS

Rankin received the call from Cairns on Wednesday. It was from Detective Sergeant Hardy who he had met earlier in the year. There had been two murders of prominent people that did not add up and a suicide of their killer that did not add up. It appeared a straight forward murder suicide, but he wanted Rankin's department to investigate it. Rankin left Kennedy and Black in Brisbane and took the rest of his team to Cairns. Hardy, the senior CIB detective, met them at the airport. They shed their suits and ties, as the tropical heat was oppressive.

Hardy gave Rankin and his men a brief outline of the case as they drove to a murder scene with Doyle and Connors in the back seat of the unmarked police car. Hardy said a man and his wife were shot to death in the lounge room of their house in the city's best suburban area. The gunman had then apparently suicided in a park nearby after murdering the two people. Hardy was not supporting this theory, as there were a number of inconsistency's in the case. That was why he wanted Rankin's department involved.

The known details of the deaths were, a bank manager, John Burton, and his wife, Gloria, had been shot in their lounge Saturday night. The murderer was assumed to have then killed himself in a park nearby.

The Burtons' bodies had been discovered by their daughter Sunday morning. She was a school teacher living in Innisfail and she had come to visit her parents. She was in hospital suffering severe shock. The bodies had been taken to the morgue after forensic had finished their work. The suspected murderer had been found in the park Sunday morning by a policeman on his way to work. Hardy gave Rankin the police photo of each crime scene. At the Burton house were two uniformed police and the murder scene had been taped off. The team entered the area after suiting up.

The victims had been shot in the back of the head. The police photos showed that the exit bullet had almost destroyed their faces. They had lain crumpled on the lounge, blood, brains and gore were still on the lounge and carpet. The smell of death lingered in the room.

Connors and Doyle were uneasy. Rankin was holding himself in, as was Hardy. The team inspected the house, which was on a corner block and had four main entries – back and front door, two-car garage with a door leading into the house, and a side laundry door leading to the yard and Hills Hoist.

They inspected the ground beneath the bottom windows of two story brick home. All were flyscreened and the security screens were intact. The laundry door was locked and had a locked security door in front of it. The back door and security door was unlocked. The victims were in the lounge at the front of the house.

The killer would have got to them from the back door with their backs to him.

He shot the manager and his wife in the back of the head. Hardy had the lounge and all doors dusted for fingerprints.

Forensic had now established that the same gun had killed the Burtons and the man in the park. The forensic officer, Thomas, had done an examination of the bodies and recovered the bullets from the room walls. They had gone through the victims and into plaster board of the walls of the lounge. The bullets matched the gun found beside the man in the park. The team went to where the suspected murderer had killed himself. A tent was over the park seat and table and police tape surrounded it. Two uniformed police stood outside the tape.

Suited up, Rankin entered the tent. The police photos showed a body slumped on the seat with his back to the table. He had a bullet hole in his right temple, the back of his head was open, and grey matter was over the table. A big revolver with a silencer lay on the ground next to the seat. Hardy stated the apparent murderer, Harry Smee was a burglar, small-time thief, fence, and cannabis dealer, and had a prison record, but it was hard to visualise him as an assassin. He was a fitter and turner when he worked.

The bank manager, Burton and his wife were discovered much later than Smee. There had been a vehicle at the park site, a Mini Cooper S. The table had been dusted for prints, as was the car, which had been confirmed as belonging to Smee.

They all went to the police headquarters. Rankin payed his respects to the area superintendent, Bowen. Hardy had set up an incident board in a room at the police station, and Rankin would work off this.

Hardy went through the known facts – two people of good standing murdered and the suicide of the assumed killer. Ballistics confirmed that the same gun had killed all involved.

All police in the area were on the case and questioning neighbours of the murdered people, their friends and Smee's know associates. Most petty criminals, known drug users, and small time drug dealers had been questioned. Clarke, one of his friends, had an interesting story. He said Smee had asked him to drive his car to the CBD and leave the key on the front tyre. He was promised twenty quid for this and was to leave the vehicle at four pm Saturday and pick it up Sunday morning, which he did. He believed Smee was picking up cannabis and did not want to use his own vehicle.

No one in the Burton area or the park had heard shots, or saw a Mini Cooper car. The shots would have been muffled as the revolver found at the suicide scene had a silencer attached to it.

Hardy said, 'I have reservations about this case but the evidence on the surface seems clear cut.'

Rankin said, 'Where did Smee get the revolver and silencer?'

Hardy said, 'Thomas had stated it was an old army thirty-eight weapon. How Smee had it was a mystery, but he could have stolen it in a burglary. The owner would not have reported it as it was an illegal weapon. The silencer was crude but efficient. He could have made it himself as he was fitter and turner.'

It was late afternoon so his team were driven to where they were staying. Rankin was driven to the morgue, gave his card to the attendant, and asked to see the principal forensic officer, Thomas. Thomas came to the door and they exchanged greetings. Thomas confirmed the same gun had killed all. The sight had been taken off and there were threads for the silencer to be screwed on. It was crude but effective. Rankin asked what prints were on the gun trigger and Thomas stated, 'Thumb prints. With the silencer, it was a long weapon.'

Satisfied, Rankin was driven to where they were staying.

It was a good, inter-town motel, owned by an ex-policeman. All rooms had a phone, but calls had to go through office. They met in the restaurant for tea and brought themselves up-to-date on what they had learned. Doyle said, 'The murderer came and left by the back doors, which was unlocked. Smee would not have had any problems with the back door locks if he is the killer.'

Doyle said, 'Why would a big cumbersome gun like the one used?'

Rankin replied, 'Might be all that was available and its bullets did maxim damage.'

Doyle asked, 'Your take on it Chief?'

Rankin said, 'At the moment, we don't know who benefits from the deaths. They will have to be investigated and the people assassinated investigated.'

Connors nodded thoughtfully. 'Chief Inspector Hardy stated they were good citizens.'

'Always remember things are not always as they seem. All involved have to be investigated, both victims and anyone suspected of murdering them.

'Don't believe what people say and saw without checking it thoroughly, even police statements,' Rankin said.

Doyle said, 'The gun and silencer would be hard to conceal here as no one wears coats.'

Rankin nodded. 'The killer could have attached the silencer inside the house.'

'Still a big weapon to hide,' Doyle added.

'Probably carried in a brief case,' Rankin suggested.

Their meals arrived and conversation ceased. Rankin went to his room and his men to a pub across the road. Rankin put a call through the motel exchange to his wife. Next morning, after an average night's sleep and a good breakfast, Rankin instructed his team to requestion all known associates of Smee and read all reports from the local investigation. The papers had screaming headlines about the murders, but had not mentioned Smee. When they found out this was a murder and the killer suicided they would have gone on to other stories after a few days, but when Rankin's presence was noted there would be an influx of southern reporters and TV people. The State Homicide Department in the area meant something big was happening.

At police headquarters, Hardy gave Rankin further information on the murdered Burton. He had managed the bank for a decade, was a member of Rotary, golf club, and racing committees.

His wife, Shirley, was a retired nurse but on call if needed. She was a member of many women's clubs and Rotary inner wheel organization.

Burton had two sons, both bank managers in outer Brisbane and a daughter, Margaret, who discovered the bodies. Margaret was a first year school teacher in Innisfail.

Rankin asked Hardy, 'What are your private feelings about this case?'

Hardy said, 'On the evidence presented, the coroner will find murder-suicide, but there too many inconsistences in this case.'

Rankin nodded. 'I agree, but the facts will agree with the coroner findings. The main question now is the gun's origin. I believe it was the only one available that could not be traced. Bullets for it would be hard to get, but could have been as old as the weapon. But why murder the Bartons. Is there anyone living in the area that warrants police attention?'

'No. It's snob hill. Professional people and the wealthy live there.'

Rankin rose from his seat. 'Let's go for a drive.' The press was at the station fence and yelled questions at them as they drove from the police yard. Rankin asked Hardy to drive around the area of the murders. It was an area of expensive brick houses. The Burton two-story home was on a corner block, opposite a similar home that had CCV in front of it and on both sides. Rankin asked Hardy to drive past this house and both noticed the back of the house also had CCTV coverage.

Rankin asked Hardy who owned and he answered, 'Bruno Grasonof who is a very wealthy Italian.'

They drove back to the station and through the press, who again threw questions at them.

Rankin had been deep in thought on the drive back. At the incident room, with his men absent requestioning Smee's associates, Rankin went to his white board and wrote Burton's neighbour's name, Bruno Grasonof.

Marker poised, Rankin asked, 'What is known about this man?'

Hardy said, 'Owns two coffee shops, a big restaurant, two cafes, and is a big bookie with a big illegal SP shop. All are solid businesses, and he employs heavy security guards. He is suspected of being into cannabis dealing, which is now big business here. Once a cottage industry but now a big commercial enterprise.'

Rankin said, 'His businesses appear sound. Why get involved with drugs?'

'Three boys put through the best boarding colleges. One now at university, two still at expensive boarding schools, and two girls at an expensive girl's college must put a strain on his other business.'

'Good Catholic man?'

'With an incubator wife,' Hardy said, 'Cowley, in charge or the drug squad here, would give you the details of Bruno,'

Rankin thanked him for the information and then asked, 'What's Bruno's home address?' Hardy gave it to him and Rankin noted it on the white board.

'Have you established who benefits from the death?'

Hardy said, 'I know the Burtons' solicitor well and have that information. Two sons in Brisbane, both bank managers and daughter in Innisfail, four sisters in Sydney on Shirley's side.

All who benefit are being questioned about their whereabouts at the time of the murders by police.

Rankin said, 'You are very efficient, Inspector. Now to the character of the victims, starting with John Barton.'

'Plays golf with our superintendent and Mayor – wife's on committees with my wife.'

Rankin decided not to pursue the matter any further for the moment.

He and his men met at the open beer garden at the pub across from their motel at one pm as arranged.

They all agreed that Smee's associates were tight-lipped but did not seem to mourn Smee's passing. Clarke confirmed what he had done with his car. The woman Smee lived with, a barmaid at a rough pub, was not in tears about his demise, merely asked what would happen to his car now. But all were surprised he had assassinated two people. They did not see him in that role. All denied knowing about the gun.

No one had anything to add. Rankin ordered a round of drinks and an orange drink for himself. It was hot and humid. They ate and went back police headquarters. His men rechecked all police statements and then went to check who had left the area by plane on Sunday morning.

The Cairn's Cup was on last Saturday, a big money race meeting attracting southern punters and the city had many attractions the night of the cup. Hundreds had flown in Saturday morning, but Rankin's interest was in who flew out Sunday morning.

Rankin had formed the opinion that a hit man was involved and Grasonof was the target.

Clarke's statement to Doyle about leaving a car for Smee's use strengthened his theory. Smee took the hit man in it to the wrong house, and left Clark's vehicle for the hit man to use. The wrong people were assassinated. The hit man had realised his mistake, carried out the action to complete his plan and close the circle by killing Smee as planned, and making it appear murder suicide. He left the area as soon as possible. There would not be a large number of people on Sunday's planes, as most visitors would leave Monday.

Connors rang and told him that twenty-five people had flown out Sunday and he had their names and addresses. Back at the station, Rankin faxed them to Commissioner Wirth, who would have them investigated by CIB and uniformed police. Rankin now had a solid theory of what could have happened.

He updated the incident board with the statement of Clark leaving Smee his car. The car had gone to forensics. No residue of cannabis was located and the only prints were Smee's and Clark's.

'Whatever Smee wanted the car for it was not to transport cannabis,' said Harvey.

Rankin said, 'My men have checked who was on the plane that left here on Sunday morning and the information had been sent to Brisbane police.'

'What's your theory?' Hardy asked.

'A professional hit man did the killing, and Smee was the message boy, and also a victim.'

Hardy nodded thoughtfully. 'That's drawing a long bow, but it makes more sense than Smee being the killer.'

'The hit man had been given the wrong address for Bruno Grasonof, who I believe was the target. A photo of either house would look the same if the killer had one. Smee would not have been in on a murder plot, but was probably told there was a safe in the house full of money after the big race meeting, and the hit man was going to rob it. He wanted a gun with a silencer, as he might have had to put shots into the wall to frighten Grasonof.

'The arrangement must have been made long before the murders. Smee had jail contacts, and would have had to secure the weapon and make the silencer. He was to ensure the back door was open and then go to the park and wait, expecting a big payoff. The gunman would have been shown photos of Bruno, but when he examined the faces of the people he shot, he would have realised his mistake but still carried out his agenda and killed Smee as planned.

'This made it look like murder-suicide, got rid of the gun and allowed him to escape. The car Smee's friend had supplied was used by the killer, then left as was arranged. Smee could have been with him when he surveyed the Barton house earlier.' There was silence in the room.

He asked Hardy to get Crowley from the drug squad to their station. He was told he was on a drug raid and would be available tomorrow morning. It was late in the afternoon and Rankin called it a day. He and his team went to the beer garden of the pub across from their motel, ordered drinks, and discussed what they had discovered. It had been an eventful day. Rankin used the station phone to ring Wirth and his wife.

After breakfast next morning, they pushed through the gathering press and TV crews at the police fence and gate. Four uniformed constables were inside the fence. Rankin and Hardy gathered at the incident room. Connors and Doyle went through all the police statements taken.

Rankin went through the events of yesterday and they agreed with him that a hit man had got the wrong address and killed the wrong people. Detective Sergeant Crowley joined Rankin and Hardy in the incident room. Rankin asked for a run down on Bruno Grasonof.

Crowley stated, 'Bruno is a big, fearless bookmaker, respected business owner, owns cafes, fruit markets, buildings, and a classy restaurant.'

Rankin said, 'And a big SP illegal, betting business.'

Crowley said, 'You will have to ask Superintendent Bowen about that,' and continued, He is a big donor to his church and many worthy causes, but I suspect him of controlling the distribution all cannabis grown commercially from Cooktown to Ingham and on the tablelands. I believe he is a middle-man buying direct from major growers and selling it on to wholesale buyers. Always at arm's length from the operation.'

Rankin asked, 'Who would benefit if he died for any reason?'

'If for health reasons there could be a violent aftermath. At the moment, everything is well-run and reasonably peaceful. With him gone, the drug area is leaderless and different groups will want to run it. Gang wars would result.'

'Would anyone be prepared to assassinate him?'

'Whoever did would have a well-planned take-over strategy. Our fear here is mother heroin. Bruno had a fear of it, as have most parents, and advised me of any coming into our area that he is aware of, but his distribution network could be used to get it into circulation from here. Our coastline is wide open here and it could be brought in by boat.'

'What are his known personal habits away from his businesses?'

'Saturday, he fielded at the Cup meeting. He is a fearless bookmaker and punters can get set for any amount with him. Saturday night, he was home with the wife after a big race day. All his businesses have managers as has his restaurant.'

'Money available at his house?' asked Rankin.

Crowley said, 'Would be very little. His bookie's bag is given to an armoured car after the races, all money from other businesses is collected Saturday afternoon and held in his safe at his restaurant, guarded by security guards until it is banked Monday. Sunday he usually goes to ten o'clock mass at the Catholic Church with his family, but the boys and girls are away and only his wife now goes with him. The rest of the day is resting, mainly at home. None of his businesses open Sunday. Probably sleeps all afternoon and he and his wife have tea and watch TV until they go to bed.'

Rankin asked, 'What does his wife do?'

'Runs the coffee shops.'

'Would she know about the drugs being handled?'

Crowley shook his head. 'I very much doubt it.'

'Will you beat this drug problem?'

'Like King Canute, I stand trying to halt it, but as long as there is a public demand for it, it will grow and flourish.'

Rankin thanked him and he left to push through the press scrum outside the police station. He turned to Connors and Doyle. 'Bring Grasonof in.'

Hardy said, 'He will refuse to come and call Sinclair his solicitor.'

Rankin said, 'He is required here as a murder target and we believe he can assist us with our investigation into the Burton murders. If he refuses to cooperate, he will be charged with impeding and obstructing a murder investigation. He will be given the choice of coming here voluntary or in handcuffs.'

'Sinclair, his solicitor, will be called by him and he is trouble.'

Rankin shrugged. 'Sinclair is not above the law and could be charged jointly with Grasonof if he hinders this investigation.'

Hardy said, 'You play hard-ball Chief Inspector.'

Rankin nodded. 'Where necessary.'

Connors and Doyle arrived back at the station. Connors said, 'Grasonof and his solicitor will be here shortly.'

'What was Grasonof's reaction to your call?'

Doyle said, 'Stunned and incredulous that it was a serious situation. He demanded his solicitor be with him at the station.'

A desk sergeant brought Grasonof, a portly, thick-set man, to the incident room. A tall, sallow-faced man was with him. The portly man said to Hardy, 'What's this about, Tom?'

Hardy indicated Rankin. 'Chief inspector Rankin called this meeting.'

The sallow-faced man said, 'I am Mr Grasonof's legal reprehensive and will be writing to the Police Commissioner about the way my client was threatened by two men from your squad, Chief Inspector.'

'Your name?' Rankin responded calmly.

'William Sinclair, solicitor.'

Rankin nodded. 'Sit down, Mr Grasonof, and Mr Sinclair.' He pointed to chairs opposite him.

Sinclair said, 'You don't have to say anything, Bruno. I will report you were intimated here by three police officers.'

Rankin said, 'I am conducting a murder investigation and it concerns your client, so please shut up and listen.' He pointed to the incident room blackboard he had set up and said, 'Anything of interest, Mr Grasonof?'

Grasonof frowned as he studied it. 'My address is there.'

'Yes,' Rankin said, 'Above it is the address of the murdered Bartons. Notice anything else, Mr Grasonof.'

Grasonof shrugged. 'We have the same type of house and corner blocks.'

'Why would someone want to kill you, Mr Grasonof? I believe you were the killer's target. A hit man was given the wrong house.'

Grasonof's dark face whitened. Sinclair went to say something, but Grasonof silenced him and said, 'Why would Smee want to kill me?'

Rankin said, 'Smee was only a message boy and a victim too.'

Sinclair said, 'It's been stated that Smee killed the Barton's then suicided.'

Rankin said, 'Not by me or any member of my squad.'

Bruno had recovered his composure and said, 'If the killer was not Smee, who was it?'

'A professional hitman. Smee's only part was to ensure entry to the back door of the house and to wait in the park where he expected to get a payoff. He did – a bullet in the head. And his death was made to look like a remorseful suicide. He did not know the assassinations were planned, possibly thought it was a robbery job. But you were the killer's target and will be again. Only, we can save you by putting the people who want you dead away.'

Bruno said, 'Who are they?'

'We don't know yet, but you must help us if you want to live. Now who has been contacting you about a distribution of heavy drugs?'

Sinclair slammed the table and said, 'You are making preposterous assumptions about my client.'

Rankin shrugged. 'Your client is free to leave. We have carried out our obligation and warned him of the danger he is in.'

'Can I have some time with my solicitor,' Bruno asked.

Rankin sent them to another interview room. Hardy said, 'You really rocked Grasonof with your statement of events. He was really scared.'

'He should be. He is walking dead unless he helps us. The people who want him dead will try again as soon as things here cool down.'

Bruno and Sinclair returned to the incident room and Sinclair said, 'My client will assist you in any way he can, but is not associated in drugs in any way. That must be understood.'

Rankin said, 'I again ask you, Mr Grasonof, were you contacted by someone about heavy drug distribution.'

'Yes, but I didn't know what he was on about.'

'Were you threatened?'

Bruno nodded, his face grim. 'Yes.'

Hardy said, 'You didn't come to us for help.'

'I have my own people to handle this.'

Rankin said, 'But do you know who the enemy is?'

Bruno shook his head.

Hardy frowned. 'We don't want a gang war here, Bruno'.

Grasonof said, 'Neither do we, but we were prepared for one here, but don't know who the enemy is.'

'How and when were you contacted?' Rankin asked.

'Late at night at home after I closed the restaurant.'

'How many times and when did it start?'

'About a month ago. He rang three times, a well-spoken man. Telecom traced the call to a Sydney public phone.'

Black said, 'Telecom gave you the information?'

'Money opens most doors,' Bruno said dryly.

'I will require dates and times of the calls,' Rankin said.

Sinclair said, 'I have them, we assumed you would require them. My client has answered all your questions and should be free to leave.'

Bruno said to Rankin, 'Anything I can help you with, just ring me. There is something else you should know – the caller was probably brought up a Catholic. The last time he rang, he said to keep myself in a state of grace if I didn't want to do business with him.' He and Sinclair left the room.

Later, Rankin said to Conners, 'What is a state of grace?'

Connors, a Catholic said, 'Go to confession, receive absolution, do penance for your sins and you are in a state of grace and ready to meet your maker.'

'The Greek saying, the enemy of my enemy is my friend, applies here. Bruno needs us and we need information from him,' Doyle said.

Rankin asked for Crowley's contact number. He rang him and told him what Bruno Grasonof had said. 'And he believed our theory of what happened. Especially the bit about him being the target.'

Crowley said, 'The people who ordered the hit would have had everything in place for a takeover, just waiting for word of Grasonof's death. Then the hit man would have advised someone when he was not assassinated and the takeover would have to be aborted.'

'He could pay a penalty for two reasons the inconvenience he caused with the takeover operation aborting and the heat he had caused by assassinating the wrong people. They would have accepted the heat from the Bruno hit, but not from the Burton murders.' Rankin said. 'If the operation was undertaken, where would it have been mounted if it was not Queensland? I have made calls to the head of the state CIB and Drug squad and confirmed they had no knowledge of it.'

'Townsville would be the logical place. Guns bought and no permit needed. Vehicles hired and men placed in position and waiting for confirmation that Bruno was dead. When that was not confirmed, the vehicles would have been returned and guns sold back at a loss, as they were illegal over the QLD border, and the operation aborted.' Rankin thanked him them and went to Hardy's office.

Hardy was in. Rankin knew he would only leave the office if something important came up requiring his presence. He would oversee everything from here. He brought Hardy up to date on events. Rankin told him, 'It will be a CIB operation from here on and I will ask the commissioner to authorise it.' He thanked him for his help and told him the people on the plane list had been cleared. They shook hands and parted.

Rankin was finished here and he and his team had to wait for a late night plane. He went back to the motel, settled with the owner, and rang Wirth, who was not available. He went to the beer garden opposite with his men and ordered drinks. As he sipped his orange drink, they went over what had happened here and considered they had covered all bases.

It was now up to CIB and Drug Squad. He had hardly used the incident board as this case flowed easily.

They spent the hour before his flight, drinking steadily in the tropical heat. They arrived in Brisbane at eleven pm, and his team went to their homes. He went to his office, checked his in-file, then got his police car, with the new mobile car phone in it, from under the station, and drove home.

He had rung his wife and said he would be late and would eat tea on the plane. The house was in darkness, only the front porch light was on. He showered and went to bed. His wife was sound asleep. He had breakfast with his family. The boys were excited he was home, but his wife was indifferent. After breakfast, they were taken to school in his wife's car, as it was on the way to where she worked as teacher. After they left, he got the morning paper from his lawn.

The Cairns' murders were on the front page. The police in Cairns had issued a press statement confirming murder and suicide. Soon it would be yesterday's news. It reported that a Cairns' businessman had been brought in for questioning, but it was in relation to a business matter, not the murder inquiry.

Rankin drove to his office and got an appointment with the commissioner. At the appointed time, he went to his meeting with the commissioner. Rankin gave him his and his team's reports. When both were finished, Wirth said, 'Good work in Cairns, Virgil. Our CIB, drug squad, and the head of the Sydney drug squad and CIB are working on the case. Turner will keep you informed.

'For your information; a known hit-man was murdered four days after the Cairns' murders.'

Rankin now knew his theory on the Cairns' murders could be right, but it would have to be put on the back burner for now. There were some killings under investigation, but nothing serious.

Turner rang him and brought him up to date on Crowley's theory about a takeover of Bruno's suspected drug business. Six men from Sydney had flown in on separate flights, but left together the day after the Cairns murders and suicide. They had bought guns and hired three vehicles. They told the gun shops they were going crocodile shotting in the far north, but returned them the next day and said it would be too wet, as the monsoon season had started. They returned the vehicle, sold back the guns, and flew out of the state together.

Prints on the guns belonged to known criminals and they were contacted by New South Wales police, as were their associates. They admitted they had been to Queensland for a holiday and had used assumed names, as they did not want to alert Queensland police that they were in the state. They were going Croc shooting, which was still legal but under attack by animal rights groups. The monsoon season meant heavy rain was coming so they called the venture off and returned to Sydney. They all worked for a Darcy Molloy, who ran a security firm employing only ex-service men. Molloy was educated. He had attended good catholic colleges, but had chosen a life living on the edge of crime.

He and his men were security guards at illegal casinos, Big SP betting shops, and handled anyone who tried to muscle in on them.

Their main employer was a merchant banker, Abel Goldstein, who lived at Potts Point. Goldstein had an extravagant lifestyle. Big yacht, private Cessna plane, and had big parties at his residence, attended by Sydney's elite, celebrities, politicians and senior police. It was the place to seen, a haven for the rich and famous. However, that has changed. Stenhouse, head of the State Drug Squad, and Egan, head of CIB, were interested in Molloy and Goldstein and now had a reason to act. Molloy and his men were interviewed and questioned about the Queensland trip.

Eagan raided their houses and found two unlicensed guns and a silencer. Stenhouse raided their homes and small qualities of drugs found. They were in the police sights. The raid upset Molloy, who sought Goldstein's help. This resulted in Stenhouse and Eagan being warned off any further investigation by the New South Wales police minister.

Stenhouse and Egan were under attack, but Stenhouse managed to get a search warrant for Goldstein's residence and yacht. Stenhouse had press contacts and informed them about this. Egan also had a warrant to search the house for suspected stolen property. They knew that if this didn't succeed both of them would be dismissed. Stenhouse was confident of finding something, but Eagan was only along to back Stenhouse. Forensic officers on the raid found residue cocaine on lounge tables, and in the bathrooms at the house and in the saloon of the yacht.

It was a small amount, but enough for the press to run headlines about drugs found in Potts Point. It was a beat up, but put the light on Goldstein and the people who went to his parties. Stenhouse had suspected Goldstein of being involved in heavy drugs but lacked proof.

Goldstein said that what had been found in his residence and yacht was easily explained. Guests must have been using cocaine without his knowledge. But the press went after him. Suddenly, his friends deserted him and distanced themselves from him.

The police commissioner stated he had attended the parties to investigate what was going on, as he had information of possible corruption. From his bolt hole, he praised Eagan and Stenhouse for their fight against crime.

Goldstein's other business arms, the casino and SP operation, were being investigated by Eagan's CIB with full press coverage. Eagan and Stenhouse believed Goldstein had gone into heavy drugs because casinos and SP betting shops were now being replaced by legal casinos and legal betting shops and that would have a big effect on the money he needed to maintain his lifestyle.

Turner concluded, 'The wash up is, both Goldstein and Molloy's men are no danger to anyone, if they ever were.'

Rankin thanked him and both wished each other a Merry Christmas.

Rankin contacted Crowley and told him he had been right about the takeover of Bruno's operation despite the lack of proof. Crowley said things would go on as normal unless Bruno fell under a bus. Then there would be much violence, as drug growers and distributors fought to control the local drug industry.

While Bruno lived, there would be peace in the valley. It was a real catch twenty-two situation.

Rankin then rang Hardy and went through the murder case with him. They agreed that the hit-man killed in Sydney was the person who killed the Burtons and Smee. And that Molloy was asked to supply the hit-man by Goldstein who then had to eliminate him for safety reasons, as Eagan put pressure on him and his crew. The coroner would find murder-suicide and then case would go on their backburner. After wishing each other a Merry Christmas, they hung up.

Rankin contacted Wirth and told him his squad had nothing serious to act on and he wanted time off. Wirth said to be back on duty the first of February.

Rankin rang a car dealer he had helped in the past and told him he wanted to rent a modest car for about six weeks. The dealer said he had a four-year-old Holden in good condition and he could pick it up tomorrow morning. Rankin did not think their old car was up to the long trip he planned to take. He dropped his police car keys at the main office and asked the sergeant there to have someone start his car weekly. He did not want to come home to a flat battery. He got a police constable to run him home.

School had broken up the day before and Rhonda was at a breakup gathering. The boys would be down at their milk bar hangout. At tea time, he told the family what he wanted to do. Leave the day after tomorrow and drive south. The boys were for it, but Rhonda said, 'What about Christmas?'

He said, 'We will have it where we are at that time. Our families can do without us.' The boys were excited and Rhonda silent.

Next morning he picked up the car and asked what he owed the dealer, who said he would invoice if he remembered. Rankin went to their bank and arranged money for the trip. It was lunch time when he got home. The boys examined the hire car. Rhonda had a parcel in the lounge, which she told him to open. In it were four loud floral shirts, two pair of knee length board shorts, a pair of calf length sandals, and a panama hat. She handed him a shirt, pair of shorts, and the sandals, and asked him to try them on. He went to the bathroom and came out dressed. He said, 'I feel and look like a dill.'

She smiled. 'No, Vergil, you look like a tourist. I have arranged with one of our neighbours to collect all mail and newspapers that are delivered, and they will start our car every week and check the house. They have the house and car keys. We can leave early tomorrow morning, have breakfast at a roadside McDonalds and take pot luck with accommodation.'

They were on the road at seven the next morning. They were a happy crowd. Rankin remembered Findlay's statement about the good times being now, and he knew he would not have to look back, *they were now.*